# WHEN
# THE
# SNOW MELTS

Born in Kerala, **Vinod Joseph** is a Mumbai-based lawyer. Apart from corporate and banking law that keeps him busy, he is a keen long-distance runner, wine taster, and cricket- and film-aficionado. Even as Vinod dreams of improving his record of 5:24 hrs for a full marathon, he still spends most of his spare time on books. Vinod hones his story-telling skills by making up bedtime stories for his five-year-old daughter.

# WHEN THE SNOW MELTS

*A thriller*

Vinod Joseph

AMARYLLIS

AMARYLLIS



This edition first published 2012.

AMARYLLIS

An imprint of Manjul Publishing House Pvt. Ltd.

Editorial Office:
J-39, Ground Floor, Jor Bagh Lane,
New Delhi 110 003, India
Tel: 011-24642447/24652447 Fax: 011-24622448
Email: amaryllis@amaryllis.co.in
Website: www.amaryllis.co.in

Registered Office:
10, Nishat Colony, Bhopal 462 003, M.P., India

ISBN: 978-93-81506-11-0

Printed and Bound in India by
Thomson Press (India) Limited

*To Nisha*

# Acknowledgements

When a professional with a demanding job manages to complete a novel, his immediate family members are bound to have paid a price. *When the Snow Melts* was written over a period of around eighteen months, between 2008 and 2009. At that time, we were living in the UK and my wife Nisha put up with me as I often wrote late into the night and over weekends. Our daughter Anika, now almost five, was too young to complain and hopefully did not suffer much, but that's mainly because Nisha put in that extra bit of care to cover up for my absentmindedness and other lapses.

Some of the writing was done during my daily work commute from Basingstoke, where I lived at the time of writing, to London, a journey of around fifty miles. When I type, I tend to use more force than is strictly necessary and I did annoy more than one fellow-commuter with my noisy typing, but I was never ever asked to stop, except once when I unknowingly got into a 'quiet' compartment by mistake and started to type away to glory. I shall forever be grateful to South West Trains for giving me around hundred minutes of uninterrupted writing time every working day.

My parents have always taken great delight in my writing and along with my younger brother Manoj and sister-in-law Vishalini, form my biggest cheer squad. They have always been around, even when we were separated by thousands of miles.

I am truly grateful to Sanjana for her faith in my work and for agreeing to publish *When the Snow Melts*. Sanjana's colleagues Rashmi and Shruti supported me a lot, from editing to fixing the cover design. I am indebted to all three of them and to Amaryllis for publishing *When the Snow Melts*.

# Prologue

THE MAN WAS INEBRIATED; THERE COULD BE NO DOUBT on that score. The mild winter light was rapidly failing and sunset was not more than thirty minutes away. Not only was his long gait unsteady, he was also swinging his stick-like arms in a manner that suggested he had partaken more than a respectable quantity of the amber fluid. However, despite his obvious drunkenness, he made his way up Heathcombe Road and entered Iver Close without worrying about directions, giving the impression of being on very familiar territory. A stretch of the pavement was still covered with patches of snow and ice. He, very cautiously, proceeded by stepping on spots that were either free from the slippery slush or where the ice was mixed with sand and grit that the well-meaning local council scattered on the footpath after the very unusual pre-Christmas snowfall London had received a couple of weeks ago.

Well-off gentry occupied the semi-detached houses on both sides of the road, some of whom were yet to dismantle their Christmas lighting and other festive decorations. The type and make of cars that lined both sides of the road further confirmed that the area was inhabited by the upper middle class. BMWs and Mercs were the most common, while Toyotas, Hondas and Volkswagen Golfs also made their presence felt. Some of the courtyards still had snow on the grass, and the light reflected from the snow made everything look brighter than usual.

The new arrival did not fit into his surroundings. He was dressed in a dirty jacket that had obviously seen better days. A grey glove, most likely made of cotton, was stuffed into each of the side pockets of his jacket. Since it was very cold, one was forced to assume that the alcohol in his body was the reason why the Man had not donned his gloves. He wore a Rolex, but the long sleeves of his jacket prevented him from displaying more than a small part of it. He badly needed a haircut and a shave. His two-day-old stubble was partly grey, and the long and dirty strands on his head had a similar proportion of salt.

As the male specimen under observation stopped in front of a brown wicket gate, numbered 188 in bold black letters, the setting winter sun cast its long shadow across the road. A Ford Focus was parked right next to the gate and even a not-so-discerning-eye would have noticed the two long scratch marks on one of its metallic-grey sides. There was a dark blue van parked on the other side of the wicket gate and just like the subject under study or the Ford Focus, it didn't belong there either. However, the Man didn't notice any of this.

Opening the wicket gate with an unsteady hand, he took out a key from his bulky jacket. Slowly, he walked along the five concrete slabs that bifurcated the courtyard and climbed the steps in front of the door. Fluffy snow, not more than an inch thick, covered the courtyard. Short stems that protruded from the blanket of snow suggested that the place was unkempt and would not have been a pretty sight if not masked by the snow. It was dark in the porch and a sentinel light came on, triggered by the human presence. The Man looked relieved. He was tall and his head nearly touched the top of the door. Though unnecessary, he stooped a little as he entered the house.

The moment the Man opened the door, two men wearing thick, padded jackets and leather gloves got out of the dark blue van and rushed into the house. The victim didn't notice the men behind him till it was too late to slam the door shut.

'If only you didn't drink too much, you wouldn't be in so much trouble,' one of the two men smirked.

'You have no right to enter my house without my permission,' the Man retorted, his hands angrily bunched into the pockets of his jacket.

'Like hell we don't have permission! You should have thought of this before borrowing money from Tiny Tim. In any case, we didn't force entry, did we, old chap? You opened the door for us, didn't you?'

'Get lost,' the Man told the two men, without conviction.

'Tsk, tsk! Is this how you welcome us when this is our first visit in the New Year?'

'Happy New Year then. Now please leave.'

'Let's get down to business, shall we? You were planning to go back to the shit-hole you came from without repaying the two thousand pounds you owe Tiny Tim. Did you think you would get away with it?'

'What makes you think I was planning to leave?' the hapless victim spluttered. 'Do I look like a man about to leave the country?'

'I don't know and I don't care. Tiny Tim thinks you are about to flee. Do you have the dough?'

'But I have till the end of next week!' The protest against such injustice sounded like a howl.

'You were planning to fly away tomorrow. So, it is due *now*!'

The Man was silent. After a thoughtful pause, he spoke, 'I need time. I have arranged for money. I'll pay Tiny Tim in a week's time. There's no way I can pay him now.'

'I don't think Tiny Tim has any faith in your ability to pay him back. He has asked us to collect the money right now. Today. Now!'

'I just don't have the money,' the object of our scrutiny said.

However, the two men did not seem to be put off by it. 'Never mind, old chap, we'll take something else then. Don't you worry.'

The Man remained silent. His face showed a mix of anger and wonder.

'Now, sir, if you could hand over your Rolex...' the younger of the two men said politely. The two men hadn't taken off their heavy jackets or gloves, possibly because the room, like the rest of the house, was unheated.

'How do you know I am wearing a Rolex?' L'Homme stood with his hands limp by his sides. By now, the sleeves of his jacket went a little beyond his wrist, hiding the Rolex very well.

'Do you want to give it to me or shall I take it?' threatened the older man.

'If you want it so badly, you can have it.' Wrapping the last remnants of his self-respect around him, the prey took off his Rolex, and gave it to the younger man. The older man took one look at the watch and declared, 'Eddie, this one's fake!'

'Well, the real one is with a pawnbroker. If you gents could lend me five thousand quid, I can get it for you.'

'Bob, shall we take his laptop and his TV?' the younger man asked, casually dropping the fake Rolex into his pocket.

'The TV belongs to the landlord,' the Man demurred. 'Practically everything belongs to the landlord. You'll get into trouble if you touch any of his things.'

'Is that right, sweetie?' said Bob as he casually punched the Man in his tummy causing something more than mild discomfort. As the quarry's face contorted in pain, the men walked around the room.

'We ought to just smash up the TV,' declared Eddie. He then turned around and asked with mock concern, 'If we do that, will your landlord come after us? Or will he take it off your deposit?'

He remained silent, defeat writ large on his middle-aged face.

Eddie made his way to the kitchen, leaving the Man with Bob. A few seconds later, he called out, his voice laced with disappointment: 'Bob, the fridge is empty!'

'Nothing at all?' Bob yelled back, sounding equally crushed.

'A takeaway box; some curry inside. Some pasta. Tomatoes. Cheese. Jam. Two bottles of water. Not much.'

'Any beer?'

'Not even a drop!'

'Where have you hidden the booze?' Bob asked his prey only to be met with silence.

'Where's the booze? It must be somewhere,' Bob directed his question at Eddie as he walked around the living room. The chest of drawers near the television looked as if it contained books and other stuff. Bob opened it carelessly to reveal a set of five liquor bottles, one of which was almost empty.

'Eddie, the booze's here!'

'Any of it good?' Eddie asked as he walked over.

'I don't know. Five bottles of the same kind. What's this, my friend?' Bob held up a bottle that was almost empty. He read out the words on the label slowly. 'Old Monk. This good?' he asked the Man.

'Some like it. Why don't you try it?'

Bob held the bottle to his lips and took a small sip suspiciously. Bob grimaced violently. 'Not for me! Eddie, you wanna try?'

'No, it might have something in it. Never heard of it. Old Monk?'

'It's just rum. Made in India,' the owner of the Old Monk bottles responded coolly. 'You could have it with cola, but then you'll be called a sissy.'

'Shut up!' yelled Eddie. The Old Monk drinker shrugged his shoulders in response. He obviously didn't mind Bob and Eddie not taking a liking to his liquor.

'Well, you can keep your booze. We don't want it. You ought to be grateful.' If Eddie expected a volley of gratitude, he was disappointed, but not for long.

'Hello! Isn't that a car key?' Eddie shouted, as he walked over to the small dining table that occupied one end of the living room. He picked up the car key that lay carelessly on top of the table.

'The Ford Focus outside is yours, inn't it?'

'I bought it on a loan. Stopped paying the bank after the first two instalments.'

'We'll take it nevertheless,' reaffirmed Bob.

'Listen, I can give you guys a cheque for two thousand pounds.'

'Ummm, aaaah, with due respect, sir, your creditworthiness ain't very high right now.'

'Where's your laptop?'

'I've pawned it.'

Bob gave an exasperated grunt. 'I give up,' he confessed in a manner that suggested he was nevertheless enjoying himself immensely. He and Eddie went outside. Their victim followed them, shutting the door behind him.

Eddie eyed the unwashed Ford. 'I guess it would have been too much to expect you to wash your car once in a while? We have car washes in this country, you know.'

'I doubt if this will fetch two thousand quid,' Bob wondered aloud. The three men stood on the deserted road. The sun had almost set by then, but streetlights lit up the entire road in a soft yellow glow.

'It was bought with a loan. Most of it is outstanding. If you take it away, the bank will be after you,' warned the not-so-proud owner of the car.

'It really like banks. I *so* love them,' smirked Bob. 'Now *you* listen to me. If you report this car as stolen, we'll come back and kill you. You just keep paying back that car loan, nice and easy, okay? Wherever you are! Every month! Okay? If you can, that is. If you can't, never mind. Banks are no good at getting their money back. But don't ever report this as stolen. 'kay?'

'What the heck, Bob?' exclaimed Eddie. 'This bastard is planning to run away. He'll be out of this country within a few hours' time. He should be giving us all he has before he leaves for good!'

All that was too much for the Man; in a sudden unexpected burst of energy, he rushed at Bob, and head-butted him in his stomach. Bob went down like an axed pole. Eddie took out a Smith & Wesson revolver from inside his jacket, but before he could use it, the Old Monk drinker kicked it out of his hand with a speed that was even more surprising, considering the state of drunkenness he was in not so long ago. The revolver clattered and fell ten feet away on a clump of snow. Before Eddie could recover, the Man punched him on this chin with a left hook and sent him reeling backwards. Three seconds later, the fake Rolex was back on the wrist it belonged to.

Bob got up unsteadily and stood with one hand on the Ford, using it as a support. He put his hand into his jacket.

'Don't,' warned the hunter who, until a short while earlier, was being hunted.

Bob continued to fumble with his jacket. The leather gloves he wore hindered his efforts.

The Man, who no longer looked so helpless, walked over and clipped him behind the ear, causing him to pay obeisance to the road once again, face down. Eddie by then had recovered from the blow. Instead of trying to retrieve his revolver, he came up from behind and hit the no-longer-so-drunk Man on the nape with a sideways chop. The Man crumbled and sank to his knees. Eddie started to step backwards to make room for a decent kick, but the Old Monk drinker lunged forward and grabbed him by his legs before he could get into a suitable position. Eddie and the Man rolled on the road that was wet with melted snow.

The Jaguar that screeched to a halt less than three feet from the Man and Eddie was spotlessly clean. The two men who got out were South Asians, just like the object of our observation. Unlike the Man, they were both a lot younger and well dressed. One of them, a handsome and clean-shaven man in his late thirties, wore a very expensive overcoat that most probably came from Harrods or Selfridges and had a hair cut that was in keeping with the latest in London fashion, one without a side parting. The other man was as tall as the Old Monk drinker; but unlike the Man who was as thin as a reed, was very heavily built, sported a military style crew cut, and a thick and luxuriant beard that came up to the middle of his chest. His brown jacket did not have the expensive and elegant air as that of his friend's, but was still something he could have worn anywhere without feeling embarrassed. Both men wore gloves, the handsome man a smart black pair that went with his overcoat and the hefty man a sober blue and cream.

'What's going on here?' the dandier of the two newcomers demanded, in an accent that was clipped and very upper class, though not really native British. The Man and Eddie got off each other and stood up. Bob sat on the edge of the pavement.

'Get lost!' snapped Eddie, even though he instinctively recognised the person as aristocratic. 'We're bailiffs and he assaulted us. The cops'll be here any moment,' he added, as if that would make the two men disappear.

'They are loan sharks,' the Man told the two new arrivals.

The handsome man with the upper class accent took out a Glock 17 semiautomatic from inside his jacket and pointed it at Eddie and Bob, 'Why don't you two beat it? You got to know when you've been licked.'

'I want my gun back,' said Eddie as though he were a schoolboy demanding a chocolate from his mum.

'And I'll shoot you dead like a dog if you try to pick it up,' replied the man holding the Glock 17. As if to buttress his statement, his bearded friend took out a Beretta M9 from one of the pockets of his jacket. The Beretta M9 looked tiny in his huge palm, but was no less menacing.

Bob and Eddie looked at each other and then at their former victim. 'We're off, but if you've any sense, you'll pay Tiny Tim anyway, Guv'nor,' muttered Bob as he and Eddie got into their blue van.

The man addressed as Guv'nor muttered something to his companion, who nodded a couple of times and then ran up to where Eddie's revolver lay. He picked it up and gave it to his friend.

'This goes into the boot,' declared the handsome man to the two men sitting inside the van. He quickly walked over to the rear of the van, opened its boot and threw the revolver inside. The boot was slammed shut.

'Don't stop until you are out of sight,' he threatened Eddie and Bob, who were about to drive off.

The Man stood and watched as if this sort of thing happened every day. However, after Bob and Eddie disappeared around the corner, his expression changed to one of bewilderment.

'Do you guys do this sort of thing on a daily basis?' he asked the handsome man.

'And do you take on a couple of tough loan sharks on a daily basis?'

'I didn't have a choice.'

'We do this only for friends. After all, we are from the same neighbourhood, aren't we?'

'Where are you from?' The Man asked his new-found friends in Hindi. Suddenly, his eyes zoomed in on the number plates of their car. 'Wait a minute, those are diplomatic plates!'

'Yes sir, I plead guilty.' The dapper dude was charm personified and his Urdu was as flowery as it could be when spoken by someone from the subcontinent's upper crust. 'I am a diplomat, a Pakistani diplomat.' He paused, looked at the Man from head to toe and asked, 'Why doesn't your car have diplomatic plates?'

The Man slowly shook his head. 'How long have you known about me?' he asked the diplomat who had just saved him from some serious trouble.

'A long time. A very long time, my friend. You need some help don't you?'

The Man pursed his lips and was silent.

'Come on. According to the met department, we can expect more snowfall this evening. Let's not stand here in the cold. Let's go to High Street and find a pub. We all need a drink, don't we? Mind you, my friend doesn't drink at all, but he doesn't mind watching others drink.'

'Do I have a choice?' asked the Old Monk drinker.

'No,' replied the handsome man. 'None at all, I'm afraid. None of us do. Everything is preordained. Inshallah.'

# 1

IT IS NOT EVERY DAY THAT A 'veteran spook' gets to defect to the enemy. I woke up to the shrill clamour of my timepiece that morning. Normally, I wouldn't have needed an alarm to wake me up. However, I had been nervous, irritable, tired and sleeping very badly for the past few weeks, if not months and so, just to play safe, I had set the alarm for seven-thirty. I was glad I did.

I splashed some warm water on my face and looked in the mirror. I hardly recognised the puffy but thin face with bloodshot eyes that stared back at me. The stubble on my face was a couple of days old and it looked and felt much older as I rubbed my hands across my cheek. A shave wouldn't be a bad idea, I thought. I had been regular at shaving until a year ago. By the time I got dressed and out of the house, it was almost eight-fifteen. I was supposed to be standing outside Uxbridge tube station at nine-fifteen. On a normal working day, the District Line would take me from Hammersmith to Westminster and from there, I would walk to the Foreign and Commonwealth Office. Today was Defection Day and I planned to take the Piccadilly Line – that went in the opposite direction.

There had been some snowfall over the past few days, which was excessive by London standards. The snow lay piled on footpaths. I was a bit nervous thinking about whether the Piccadilly Line would run a normal service; on its western run, it goes overland after Earl's Court and London's transport systems aren't really geared for anything more than a dusting of snow. I was right, the Piccadilly Line tube was experiencing some 'minor' delays, as described by a lady with a Caribbean accent who repeated her announcements over the public address system every couple of minutes; but I still managed to reach Uxbridge at ten past nine.

I was dressed in a pair of scruffy jeans and the only jacket I still possessed, something that used to be a dark shade of grey and had seen better days. My backpack was in the same state as my jacket and if the world-famous shoe makers whose brand name was displayed in small faded letters across it had got to know of its existence, they would probably have approached the courts for an injunction to prevent me from using it in public and disgracing their brand name and reputation. Only my dark blue gloves looked much better and I could have worn them anywhere, but that was because they weren't really mine. I had found them on a park bench the day before and they had fit my hands to a T. I had thought that it would be churlish to turn down such an unexpected bounty.

Just outside the station, I found a café that looked quite inviting. I went in and bought a Danish pastry and a cappuccino. The café was nearly empty except for a couple of workmen with big splotches of paint on their trousers and overalls; they were eating rolls and drinking tea from oversized mugs. If it hadn't snowed, they would have been standing outside, leaning against the wall and whistling at women walking past – they were those kind of workmen. I sat at a table not far from them, my backpack on my lap, ate what I'd bought and took intermittent gulps of the bitter cappuccino.

There were Tubes entering and exiting the station every minute or so. This was peak hour when office goers and school kids crammed into all modes of public transport. Uxbridge was the end point for both the Metropolitan Line and the Piccadilly Line and I wondered who would be coming over to meet me. Would it be Ayub? I doubted it. The Pakistanis were fatalistic, believing that everything was predestined and preordained. In effect it meant they wouldn't take the most basic of precautions and would end up in hot water in circumstances that are very much avoidable. However, Ayub was an Oxford graduate, a man who had lived in the West for over fifteen years. He was unlikely to be so foolhardy. No, he wouldn't turn up in person to collect me, I thought.

When I had stuffed the last of the Danish pastry into my mouth and finished my cappuccino, I walked out of the café. Junaid was waiting outside the station, accompanied by a man with a neatly trimmed goatee. I had nearly forgotten how huge Junaid was and how lengthy and bushy his beard looked. Dressed in a loose-fitting dark blue jacket that was very clean, unlike mine, and had obviously been bought very cheap, again unlike mine, Junaid looked very menacing as usual. His companion on the other hand was middle-aged and had a paunch. He seemed to be one of those men who manage to look absent-minded and constantly proclaim to the world that they are intellectuals.

It was twenty past nine. I wiped my right hand on my trousers and went forward to meet them. Junaid seemed disappointed with me. At least, the frown on his face seemed to suggest so. Instead of coming forward, he avoided eye contact and stood where he was while his companion trotted forward.

'Can you tell me how I can get to Brunel?' he asked me.

'Brunel? As in the university? Don't have a clue, mate.'

'Oh! I have a map, but it doesn't show Brunel. Can you please take a look?'

'Why not?' I was slightly impressed. This was not fatalistic behaviour. Rather, it was very professional, much more professional than I was feeling at that moment.

As I expected, the map that was almost shoved into my face had the following typewritten at the bottom:

'Take the Metropolitan Line to Aldgate. Not Aldgate East. Aldgate. Wait outside the exit.'

'This is where Brunel is,' I told the Man with the goatee, pointing to a random spot on the map.

'Oh, I see. That seems a walkable distance. Or should I take a taxi?'

'It would take fifteen minutes or so, I'd say.' My fingers traced a line from Uxbridge Tube Station to a car park and from there to the spot I had picked earlier. I was sure that Brunel University was nowhere in the vicinity of that spot. Thankfully there was no one else within earshot who could hear the rubbish I was mouthing. 'Why don't you walk this way and then, once you get to this car park there, ask someone for directions?'

'Thank you so much.' I didn't wait to respond. Instead, I strode back to the station in the manner of a man in hurry. I went to the ticket machine and bought a ticket to Aldgate, in zone one. It was a pity I couldn't travel on my oyster card which had plenty of credit left in it, but that would have left a trail as clear as the oyster card's logo, which was a white crescent in the middle of a blue oyster. I hoped I wouldn't have much travelling to do once I reach Aldgate. Why couldn't Ayub have arranged for that goateed man to give me a paper ticket to Aldgate, I wondered with a degree of irritation. Not only would I have saved some money, the cameras near the ticket machines would not have recorded my making the purchase. Wasn't I already a guest of the al Qaeda in the UK? If someone were to diligently go through tube station video recordings for that morning, they would know I had purchased tickets from Hammersmith and Uxbridge. With a bit of extra effort they would be able to work out that I had bought a ticket for zone one from Uxbridge. I shrugged my shoulders. It just couldn't be helped. Hopefully they would take a day or two to institute a proper search for me. By which time I would be safely ensconced somewhere.

I relaxed once I was inside the tube, which wasn't too crowded, thanks to the severe cold and snowfall. I was undoubtedly in the hands of professionals, even though they had forced me to pay for my tube journey to Aldgate. I was supposed to be at my desk at the Foreign Office by nine. When would they start missing me and sound the alarm? To be honest, my attendance record and punctuality hadn't been terrific in the last six months and it would be some time before anyone took notice of my absence.

The Metropolitan Line goes overland from Uxbridge till Finchley Road, where it dips underground. The view, as I looked out of the window, was straight off a soppy Christmas card. Until Harrow-on-the-hill, most of my journey was through wooded areas and meadows, which were carpeted with snow. A man sitting next to me got up and left, leaving behind the newspaper he was reading. I think it was *The Times*. I tried reading but gave up after a few minutes. I was too nervous and couldn't focus.

At Aldgate, I exited the tube station and stood for a minute. There wasn't much snow around, possibly because it was so close to the Square Mile, nay it was the eastern boundary of the Square Mile, as London's financial district was sometimes referred to. Aldgate tube station is a bit of a cul-de-sac. It's the final stop for the Metropolitan Line on its eastern end and the Circle Line, which is not very reliable, passes through it. The station itself has only one exit, which was on Aldgate High Street. From where I stood, I could see on my right, the Gherkin and the high rises of the City. To my left was the region known as Tower Hamlets, an area with a large Bangladeshi population. A few local lads, all of them obviously of Bengali origin, stood near the entrance of the tube station, giving away free copies of *City A.M.* One of them offered me a copy. I took it eagerly, expecting it to contain further directions, like a hand-written note on one of its pages. I found none.

A young South Asian man wearing a pair of blue jeans and a very cheap looking bomber jacket, possibly a Sri Lankan, came to me and asked in broken English, 'How to go to Toynbee Hall?'

'I've got no idea, mate,' I said, expecting him to pull out a map. Instead, he shrugged his shoulders and walked ahead to ask someone else.

I stood there in the cold, feeling somewhat silly and out-of-sorts. I wanted to pee. I looked at my watch. It was ten-forty. After waiting another five minutes, I went inside the tube station and asked an assistant where the men's loo was. The young lady I spoke to, a chubby and attractive Afro-Caribbean woman in her thirties, scratched her head and said, 'I donno for sure. There's one this way…' she indicated right and then said, 'you might as well go this way.' This time she indicated to the left. 'There are some restaurants there. You'll find a toilet in one of them, I guess.'

'Surely, there's a public toilet somewhere here,' I said, a trifle tersely.

The young woman was not in the least upset. 'Yes, there is one on the other side of the road. Inside the bus station over there, across the road....' She pointed her finger towards the exit. 'But it's been out of service since last evening.' She shook her head slowly, sadly. Where will you pee now, you poor you, her eyes and open mouth seemed to ask me.

'What about Fenchurch Street station? Isn't that close by?'

'Yes, but the restaurants over there are closer.' The plump arm swished to the left.

I shrugged and walked away. I reminded myself that I was in the East End, an area that had once been a slum. I had no right to expect the sort of civic amenities that the better-off parts of London had.

There was a large crowd of people waiting to cross the road. I joined them with the intention of going towards Fenchurch Street. No sooner had the lights changed and I started to cross the road when I heard a man's voice in my ear say, 'Go to Tower Hill and take the District Line towards Mile End. Wait outside the exit.' The accent was very English, the intonation that of an educated person. I did not turn till I had crossed the road. When I finally turned my head in the direction of the voice, I saw amongst the crowd, a thin, young, white man scurrying away. Was it he who had whispered in my ear?

I was impressed with Ayub's team. Even if I was being followed by anyone other than Ayub's people, my followers would have no idea what I was up to, other than that I was playing hookey. But a sense of unease began to set in. These people were professionals. It would be very difficult to get them to toe my line or outwit them at any point.

'Is there a bus towards Mile End?' I asked a young shop assistant standing outside a dry cleaning store.

'Sure. Cross the road and take bus number… 20 or 205 and maybe number 10. Any of them will take you to Mile End.'

I considered going to Mile End without taking a leak. I looked at the heavy traffic and decided not to risk that. Any bus was likely to take at least thirty minutes to get to Mile End. I made my way to Fenchurch Street station, which had a small toilet, conveniently located, not far from its entrance. It took me ten minutes to make my way back to Aldgate Tube station.

As I waited for a bus to Mile End, I could feel many eyes on me. I was sure that I was being followed, most likely by a team of people rather than an individual. Within five minutes, I saw number 205 approach the bus stop. It was one of those double-decker buses with two automatic doors, the door in front for entry alone and the door in the middle for exit. I got in, fished out some loose change, paid for my ticket and found myself a seat on the lower deck near the exit door. I shrugged and wriggled out of my backpack and placed it on my lap. Of the mob that got in along with me, two men seemed intriging. Both were very young and seemed totally uninterested in me. One of them stood behind me, his hand resting lightly on top of my seat, while the other, stood near the exit door. The bus slowly made its way up Whitechapel High Street. As it neared Whitechapel tube station, I got up, pulled on my backpack and went over to the bus driver. The two men now looked taut and ready for action.

'This bus goes to Mile End, doesn't it?' I asked the bus driver in a loud enough voice.

'Yes, it does,' said the driver, a greying veteran in his fifties; he didn't even bother to look at me.

I went back to my seat, but it was now occupied by a lady with an Afro hair-do. I stood near her and held on to the bar of her seat. The bus continued its slow crawl forward. A few minutes later, there was another stop coming up and I could see a number of people queuing to get into the bus. I slowly made my way to the driver once again. This time the two men had bemused expressions on their faces.

'Would you know when we are likely to reach Mile End?'

The driver turned to look at me, looked at his watch and seemed to be mulling over whether he should reply to my question or not. I looked at him expectantly. By that time, the bus halted at the bus stop and the doors swung open. People started to get out through the door in the middle. The entry door wasn't more than two feet to the right of the bus driver. Six or seven people started to get in through the doors. I quickly turned around and threw myself into them. There were cries of shock and anger. A middle-aged woman who might have been Filipino or Thai said 'Excuse me!' in dignified protest. I ignored them all, bulldozed my way out and landed on a pavement that was as slippery as hell.

I started to run, but soon slowed down thanks to the slush. I walked quickly along the footpath for a minute and then entered a side road on the left. I stopped for a moment to see if I had managed to lose my shadows. There was no sign of the two young men. I turned right and walked into a lane that I hoped was a route parallel to what my bus would have taken. After a few minutes, I turned right again and made my way to the main road. I hailed a prowling taxi. 'Mile End tube station please,' I said, feeling a lot better. Once I got in, I felt in control of myself; and my backpack was back on my lap.

My Blackberry sang out the opening bars of Lili Marleen. I fished it out of my jacket hoping that Ayub wasn't being rash enough to call me.

# 2

I NEEDN'T HAVE WORRIED. THE call wasn't from Ayub. Instead it was from General West. He sounded irritated, and quite rightly so. General West had called for a meeting at quarter to eleven. General Qayyum was to be there, along with half a dozen minions. If I hadn't jumped ship, I would at that moment have been sitting on one of the straight-backed chairs at the FCO, possibly sipping tea and trying not to show the effects of previous nights' excesses, as someone, possibly me, held forth on whether a particular intelligence report was spot on target or full of crap. Neither General West nor General Qayyum was used to being kept waiting, especially by their subordinates.

'Where the hell are you, Ritwik?' General West barked into the phone.

'I'm so sorry, general. I'm unwell. Thought I'd put my feet up and get some rest. I left a message on your answering machine.'

'Like hell you left a message for me. If you are ill, you are expected to report to your designated doctor. Have you done that?' There was a prolonged silence. A woman giggled. It had to be Jo. No one else could giggle like Jo. 'What's wrong with you, Ritwik? What's wrong with you, man? You are not the guy I knew until six months back.'

I could imagine General Qayyum sitting across the table from General West looking just as exasperated. General West was right. I was not the man either of them had known until six months ago. The man they had known wouldn't have dreamt of deserting.

'Listen, Ritwik, you better report your fat arse to the office as quickly as you can. Else I'm going declare you AWOL and have you dragged back. In chains if need be. We already have enough shit floating around.' With that, he slammed the phone down, before I could point out to him that since I was still an employee of the Indian government and he, an American soldier, there would be certain diplomatic niceties to be observed before he could have me arrested in the United Kingdom. To be honest, knowing General West, I knew he wouldn't give a bloody damn about diplomatic niceties and if he wanted to have me arrested, he would get his British hosts to do it quietly and without any trouble at all.

I wondered how much longer they would wait before they took action. This wasn't the first time I had failed to turn up at work or be unavailable for a scheduled meeting.

Most probably, they would send someone to my house at Chiswick to see if I was there and report back, just as they had done last time. They could pinpoint my location using the response from my blackberry, if they wanted to. I didn't think matters had reached that stage yet, but they would soon, most probably by the end of the day when someone went to my house and found that I was not lying sprawled on my couch in a drunken stupor, as had happened two weeks ago.

General Qayyum hadn't uttered a word during the entire exchange, though I was sure the phone was on speaker. Which was just like General Qayyum. A silent, taciturn and highly efficient man, he was one of General West's various right hands.

By the time my taxi reached the tube station at Mile End, it was eleven forty-five. I switched off my phone and pulled on my backpack. The goateed man stood near the entrance, looking nervous. As soon as he spotted me walking towards him, he took out his mobile phone and speaking in Bengali said, 'He's here.' The high opinion I had formed of Ayub's team just disappeared. If I were Ayub, I'd have had a bullet fired into the forehead of the goateed head. Didn't he realise what sort of risk he might be exposing me to?

To make matters worse, Junaid materialised from inside the tube station and joined the goateed man. 'We have a car waiting for you,' Junaid told me softly in Cockney English. I gave up and walked over to the unmarked Peugeot that Junaid had gestured towards with a slight movement of his hand. The snow was a lot thicker around here than at

Aldgate. The driver, a young man with shoulder-length hair and a fashionable-looking, neatly trimmed beard, gunned the engine even before we got inside. Junaid got into the front seat, while the goateed man slipped into the rear with me. The car started to move forward along the dual carriageway almost immediately. 'You've made the day for anyone who might have been following me,' I told Junaid and his friend. 'Not only am I in trouble, you guys are as well.'

The Peugeot took a U-turn and went back the way it had come, along the other side of the dual carriageway. Because of the slippery roads, it moved very slowly. The driver kept tapping the steering wheel, most probably his way of venting his frustration at the weather and the condition of the road.

'Don't worry. Nobody else has been following you,' Junaid assured me. Before I knew it, he turned towards me angrily and asked, 'But why did you take a bus to Mile End? And you ran away from the bus? Why did you?' It was obvious that Ayub hadn't taken Junaid on for his verbal ability. It was a bit funny, hearing a bushy bearded al Qaeda supporter speak with a pronounced Cockney accent.

'Claustrophobia,' I replied shortly. 'The tube makes me claustrophobic.'

'But you travelled by the tube all the way from Uxbridge?' Junaid protested.

'He is only joking,' Junaid's friend clarified. He then turned to me and said, 'I'm Munir.'

I warily shook his hand and asked, 'Where's Ayub?'

'He's waiting for you. Can you please switch off your phone?'

'Where are we headed to?'

'We'll be moving around in circles for a bit. Then we'll go somewhere. And from there we'll go somewhere else. It doesn't matter. You don't need to know that,' Munir laughingly told me. 'Are you sure your phone's been switched off? Ayub was very particular that I remind you to…'

'Don't worry. It is,' I assured him.

I looked out of the window. We had been taking a lot of left turns and it was quite obvious we hadn't gone very far from the Mile End tube station.

'All set?' Munir asked Junaid who was constantly turning his head this way and that.

'What's all set?' I asked though I had a pretty good idea of what was coming up.

'Dear Mr Ritwik Kumar, you will have to go through some minor unpleasantness.' Munir's voice was gentle. 'It's for your own good. If you would be so kind as to sit down on the floor of the car, I'll blindfold you.'

'Couldn't you guys have brought along a car with tinted windows?' I asked in exasperation. Actually, I didn't really mind and I had been expecting such a demand. If I were in their position, this was exactly what I would have done. A car with tinted windows attracts too much attention.

I took off my backpack and squatted sideways on the floor of the car, my legs facing the right door. Junaid tied a large dark blue towel around my eyes. Everything turned black. The car picked up speed and started to move in a straight line. It slowed down, turned left, and then turned right. A few more turns came up before it picked up speed again. I tried to keep track of how many left turns and right turns we were taking, but gave up after a while. I started to feel really hungry and wished I had eaten something more substantial than a Danish pastry for breakfast. More than that I wished I didn't have such long legs since I was feeling very cramped. Hopefully, the ride wouldn't last much longer as I sensed the Peugeot slow down. It inched forward and the crunching sound of gravel suggested that we were on a driveway. A door slammed shut behind us and the vehicle stopped. My blindfold was taken off.

'Get up,' Munir ordered. I didn't waste any more time sitting in that cramped space. I gripped the top of the seat in front of me and sat up. The side door was opened for me. I got out of the car without being asked to. I was inside a spacious garage. The large shutter behind me was pulled down and I had no clue where I was.

Ayub came into the garage through an open door, which probably connected the garage to the house it was a part of. 'How was the journey?' he asked.

'Horrible,' I replied. 'Can I use the loo?'

'But of course,' Ayub was all politeness, as usual. 'Before we do that, we'll have to do a quick search of you and your bag. Just to make sure...'

'To make sure of what? That I am not carrying a bomb? That I am not carrying a recording device in my jacket? That I am not lying?' I was upset and made it very obvious that I was. My face was flushed and my palms were balled into tight fists. 'If you guys are so paranoid, you ought to have maintained radio silence while bringing me here.'

'That was a mistake. A minor one.' Ayub managed to look pleasant even then. Junaid looked a trifle miffed, as if I was making a mountain out of a molehill.

'True, a minor mistake, but if things go wrong, I'll be the one taking the rap.'

Munir looked angry with me while Ayub took on a pained expression. Junaid was bemused as if trying to figure out whether we were serious or just having fun. I knew Junaid was the most dangerous of the three men. An angry outburst wouldn't upset Junaid as it would Munir or Ayub. However, if I were to make one threatening move, Junaid would react as I had seen him do earlier. For a man of such proportions, he could move surprisingly fast. A single blow from someone that size and strength could cripple a man for life, if not kill him instantly.

I didn't make any threatening moves. I just stood there like a sulking child until Ayub said, 'It won't take too long. If you could take off your jacket and allow Junaid to pat you down….'

'Junaid wouldn't want to pat me down if I were to pee in my trousers,' I said. They ignored the remark and stood waiting with polite smiles until I took off my backpack, gloves and jacket.

Junaid started to go through my jacket while Munir opened my backpack and asked. 'What's inside?'

'My toothbrush.'

'It can't just be your toothbrush. What else is in there?' Munir had a serious face and he evidently didn't see any humour in my situation.

'Something to drink. I wasn't too sure if you people would sustain me the way I need to be. Everyone has his own requirements, you see.'

Munir gingerly opened the backpack and peered inside. 'What's this?' he asked, holding up a bottle of Old Monk.

'Rum. The finest ever made. Once you get used to it, there's nothing like it.'

'Standard issue for the Indian Army, isn't it?' Ayub couldn't hide the sneer in his voice.

'Sort of.'

'I tried it once. It's actually pretty good when had with Coke.' Ayub was quickly back to being his diplomatic best.

'When mixed with Coke, it will taste like Coke. It's not a bad idea if you just drink Coke.'

'Well, once you get used to good Scotch, it's not easy to enjoy something like this,'

'Old Monk rum isn't for everyone,' I concurred.

'Three bottles?' Munir asked me.

I nodded.

'Can't have that inside the house. Sorry.' There was an air of finality about the way Junaid spoke as he continued to probe each pocket in my jacket.

'Sorry, old chap,' Ayub said, urbane as ever. 'This is Junaid's house and he won't allow liquor inside his house.'

'I could leave it outside in the garden and nip out for a drink once in a while,' I suggested.

'No.' Junaid was obviously a man who didn't waste words.

'Tell you what, I'll take it with me. You can have it back when we move you elsewhere,' offered Ayub.

'Do I have a choice?' I asked. 'Mind you, there are three bottles.' I took out my toothbrush from my backpack, shoved it into my rear pocket and handed the backpack to Ayub, who put it down in a corner of the garage.

'Three bottles and a toothbrush. That's what you've brought with you,' said Munir as though he still couldn't believe it.

'I'll take it with me when I leave,' he told Junaid.

Junaid was done with my jacket. He then started to pat me down, slowly and methodically, taking his time. 'Hurry up or I'll pee right here,' I told the men. Junaid smiled, but did not slacken his thoroughness. Finally, when he was done, Ayub returned my jacket and gloves, retaining my phone and house keys with himself and said, 'Follow me. This way to the loo.'

I followed him. Junaid and Ayub brought up the rear. 'I considered bringing a suitcase filled with three-piece suits and expensive underwear, but then I decided not to. It would have taken ages for you guys to search everything in it.'

'I asked Junaid to buy some clothes and toiletries for you. You have a jacket that we can get dry cleaned, if you like, and your shoes look like they are in good repair!'

Lunch was served for four on a table that had some cardboard snuck under two of its wobbly legs. All around me were signs of domestic life. The coffee table with a glass top that stood in between two brown sofas had a small vase at the centre. A fading red plastic rose with a missing petal, was stuck inside the vase. The remote control that lay on the windowsill had some dirt on it, possibly the remnants of food, transferred to it when used during the course of a meal by someone who ate with his or her fingers. A framed photograph of the Kabba hung on one of the walls. I looked for photographs of Junaid and his family, but didn't find any. Most probably Junaid took the Islamic injunction against photography seriously.

The food was simple but quite good. We had some dry rotis, yellow dal, chicken boti kababs and some pilaf tinted with saffron. Instead of dessert, we had lassi sweetened with mango syrup served in tall bronze glasses.

'Please compliment your wife on her cooking,' Ayub told Junaid, who gravely inclined his head.

'Yes, the food is fantastic,' I added, though Junaid didn't look particularly pleased to receive a compliment from me. He did reward me with a nod of his head though.

From what I had seen so far, I was sure that Junaid's wife would be veiled and locked up in the kitchen or bedroom. I wondered if they had any children. It didn't appear as if they did.

'I want to ask you something,' said Munir, all of a sudden. 'Wasn't there any way you could have stayed on for some more time and helped us from inside? You know, give us information and all that. Why did you have to defect now?'

'If you gentlemen could have paid me five million dollars, I would have...'

'For god's sake, stop it. Ritwik had his reasons and he has already explained them to me. Let him have his meal in peace,' Ayub silenced both of us.

We ate the rest of the meal in silence, eating the rotis with our hands and the boti kababs, dal and pilaf with a knife, fork and spoon. When we were almost through, the doorbell chimed twice. The chimes emanated from a speaker in the hall and there was no way I could figure out how far away the front door was. Junaid got up quickly, picked up a tissue and strode towards the front door, wiping his fingers as he walked forward. After Junaid shut the door behind him, I couldn't hear the sound of his footsteps anymore.

A few minutes later, Junaid came back and sat down at the table, nodding at Ayub as he did so.

'They are here, are they? How many of them?' Munir asked Junaid who held up all the fingers of his right palm, before he started to polish off the remnants of the pilaf on his plate. My heart started to beat faster. I knew who they would be. I was a professional and I knew how defectors were usually treated. I hoped that my treatment at the hands of Ayub's people was unlikely to be much different from what I had seen being meted out by R&AW to 'enemies' who defected and came over. Granted I had gone over to the pro-Taliban ISI rather that the mainstream one, but I hoped that with Ayub in charge, that wouldn't make any difference.

'Just a few friends who want to talk to you. Nothing to worry about,' murmured Ayub.

I smiled, not because I found Ayub's words comforting, but because I realised that I still thought of the side I had defected from that morning as our own boys. 'Our own boys' were pretty civilised when they debriefed defectors. But if they ever caught hold of a double agent, they were not so civilised. Every defector was suspected to be a double agent and I was sure that I too would be scrutinised to rule out such a possibility. These procedures were the same everywhere. I shuddered inside.

Ayub looked at me with concern. Had he noticed anything?

'It's nothing,' I told him before he could say a word.

# 3

THE DEBRIEFING BEGAN shortly after lunch. Ayub led me to a whitewashed room that housed a rectangular table and four men sitting around it. The room was a large one and the table and chairs took up less than one-fourth of its space giving it a bare look. Ayub and I sat down on two vacant chairs. There was no attempt at introductions, which I think was mainly because it doesn't make much sense to be introduced to someone who has his head inside a balaclava. What could you say? This gentleman here is balaclava size number 12? I assumed that like Ayub, the four men were full-time employees of the Pakistani embassy in London with diplomatic immunity. They were very courteous towards me, flattering even. Initially that is.

'It's such a privilege to meet you in person, Mr Kumar,' said one of the men, a thickset, corpulent chap, wearing a tight sweater that had shades of pink. He looked quite ridiculous. I assumed that he was the team leader, especially because he had a sheaf of papers in front of him while the others had only small notepads. 'We've heard so much about you!'

Junaid had indicated the arrival of five men. I was sure that the fifth man was recording the entire conversation from a vantage-point somewhere. I casually tilted my head to my left but saw no signs of any recording equipment. That side of the room was bare, except for some old newspapers and a large empty flower vase stacked in one corner.

'I almost met you in Kabul in 1992. You had just driven off with a bunch of your KhAD friends when we arrived.'

I smiled without saying a word. Unless I was asked a direct question, I was darned if I said anything. I tilted my head to the right and what I saw almost made me laugh. Rather than use expensive recording equipment, which could be discreetly tucked into crevices of various sorts, a rather obvious-looking recorder mounted on a tripod stood in a corner of the room. It was a rudimentary recorder, nowhere close to those sophisticated ones that relayed the recording immediately to a distant receiver.

'Let's start from the beginning,' the corpulent man ordered me in Urdu. 'Which year did you join R&AW?'

'A year after I joined the IFS. In July 1986.' To make the whole thing less boring, I decided to give names to my interrogators. What should I call the corpulent team leader? I wracked my brains for a suitable name because an inappropriate nickname could ruin the joy of being interrogated.

'The Indian Foreign Service. Do you know how difficult it is to get into the IFS?' Ayub asked the four men, keen to show that he was on my side rather than theirs. 'Every year, they take a few hundred people into the civil services of which sixteen are taken into the IFS. Sixteen out of the thousands of people who appear for the civil services exam!'

'Oh yes, we know that. What was your rank in the civil service exam?'

'I don't remember,' I said. 'It was so long ago.' The corpulent one would be Tony, I decided.

'You stood eighth, didn't you?' Tony asked me after a quick consultation with his notes.

'Yes,' I ventured after a brief pause. 'Yes, I think so.'

'You are very modest. Where were you posted when you were invited to join R&AW?'

'Moscow.'

'Your first overseas posting, wasn't it?'

I nodded my head in affirmation.

'You learnt Russian there?'

'Yes, I did.'

'How long were you in Moscow?'

'Just over a year. From May 1985 till August 1986.'

'Did you go to Kabul from there?'

'No, I went to the consulate at Dushanbe. I was there for another year.'

Tony referred to his notes once again. 'Yes, yes, you went to Dushanbe. How long were you in Dushanbe?'

I was tempted to tell Tony to cut the crap and move on. He knew more about all this than I did.

'Until July 1988.' Like beggars, defectors can't choose the questions they want to answer.

'From Dushanbe, you went to Kabul?'

'That's right.'

'That was in—'

I was forced to break my rule about not replying unless it was a direct question. 'July 1988,' I repeated.

'Yes, you said that earlier, didn't you? I'm sorry.'

'That's alright,' I was forced to say. So far, all questions had being asked by Tony. Why did they bring four men, I wondered, if Tony was to do all the talking? And where's the fifth man? I wanted to ask.

'You could speak Dari when you went to Kabul, couldn't you?'

'I had learnt Persian at college. So, it was easy to pick up Dari.' Please let your colleagues ask me a few questions, I wanted to tell Tony.

'Is that common? For Indian students to learn Persian?'

'No, very few colleges teach Persian.'

'You went to JNU, didn't you?'

'Yes.' This was getting tiresome. If they knew so much about me, why did they have to carry on in this vein?

'You did a Masters in Persian and then took the civil services exam?'

'No, I did a B.A. Honours in Persian and enrolled for an M.A. While doing the M.A., I got into the civil services.'

'Did you finish your Masters?'

I nodded and smiled, but they waited for me to say something. 'Yes, I did,' was forced out of me.

'At Kabul, you were with N.M. Ray, weren't you?'

'Yes, I was.'

'He was a clever man, wasn't he?' There was the faintest hint of a smile.

'Yes, he was a clever man.' I could have said a lot more. I could have told them that I had learnt more from Ray Sir than from any book or any other person I have worked with; that I had admired Ray Sir more than any other human being I have ever known. I was sure that my interrogator had no idea of the bile that rose to my throat as I said that Ray was a clever man. Dammit! Ray Sir had been much more than a clever man. He had been much more than a boss to me. He had been a mentor.

'Remind us, how did Ray die?'

'You know that already.' My voice was barely a whisper.

'Well we want to hear it from you.'

I started to speak wearily. I guess they wanted me to be emotionally exhausted before they got to the crucial stuff. 'When Jalalabad was under siege, Mr Ray and I went there once to talk to a few prisoners.'

'To interrogate them, you mean?'

'No, they had already been interrogated by Dostum's men.' I hid my smirk. Abdul Rashid Dostum, then a pro-Soviet, pro-Najib militia leader, who later defected to the ranks of the Mujahideen, could give even the Mujahideen and the

Taliban lessons in cruelty. 'No, there was no need for us to use any force. The prisoners were ready to talk.'

'I see. How many prisoners were there? And what did they tell you?'

'There were five men. They had been ordered to report to someone in Peshawar and from there they were to be sent to Kashmir. It was when they were trying to get to Peshawar from Jalalabad that they were captured.'

'A likely story! Why would five men be asked to leave Jalalabad when there was a war going on?'

'The fighting was almost over by then. Najib's forces had retaken Samarkhel and all the pockets around Jalalabad that had been under the Mujahideen. The Mujahideen had started to withdraw.'

'And how did your boss die?'

'Mr Ray wanted to meet a Russian adviser whom he knew well. He hitched a ride on an APC to get to where he wanted to go. We were all set to return to Kabul that day. The APC hit a mine and was destroyed.'

'So the Russians hadn't withdrawn yet?'

'No, they had, but as you know, until 1991 when the Soviet Union collapsed, there were many Russian advisers in Kabul and elsewhere.'

'Was Ray the only Indian inside that APC?'

'Yes. There were six other men, a Russian, three Tajiks, an Uzbek and a Pashtun.'

'Ray was the head of your team in Afghanistan, wasn't he?'

'Yes, he was.'

'When did you leave Kabul?'

'When you guys entered the city. Didn't you say that you just missed me as you came in?' At my insolent reply, one of the men, a slim and agile chap, with a much younger physique than Tony, whose thick moustache could be seen through the stocking that covered his face, flared up and said, 'Why don't you answer the question? You are in no position to be rude!'

'I have no wish to be rude. I am willing to tell you anything that you do not already know.'

'Just answer every question, will you?' the moustachioed man snapped. I waited for Tony to overrule his subordinate, but nothing happened. We all sat there waiting for something to happen or for someone to say something. Nothing happened. Nobody spoke. At that instant, I decided that the moustachioed one would be Rony. Slowly it dawned on me that Rony was the big boss and everyone deferred to him, even Ayub. Interesting, I thought. The boss sits around and watches while a subordinate runs the show. This was the sort of behaviour one expected from the Japanese or Koreans, but not from Indians or Pakistanis. Was Rony really younger than my corpulent interrogator Tony? Had the al Qaeda instituted a system of seniority by merit rather than age? Unlikely, but not impossible. Maybe I was wrong. Maybe the moustachioed Rony, despite his apparent agility, was actually full of wrinkles under the balaclava and was much older than Tony my inquisitor.

'I'm sorry, sir,' I told the moustachioed man, the 'sir' a concession to his Asian sensibilities which were obviously hurt.

I was a defector who was at the mercy of my interrogators.

After another minute's melodramatic silence, the man with the moustache nodded to Tony and said, 'Go ahead.'

'When did you leave Kabul?' Tony asked me again.

'Just when Najib threw in the towel and Burhan-ud-din Rabbani's men entered. In 1992.'

'Were you part of the team that took Najibullah's wife and daughter to Delhi?'

'No, I was not. I stayed on for a bit beyond that.'

'Who travelled with Najib's family to Delhi?'

I was sure they already knew, but I gave them the names anyway. Cut to the chase, mate, I wanted to tell them, but I desisted. I was surrounded by four enormous and unbelievably fragile egos. It would be so easy to piss them off and harm my prospects in the process.

'What did you do after you left Kabul?'

'I went back to Dushanbe.'

'Full-fledged diplomatic relations by then, right?'

'Yes, that's right.'

'You Indians moved fast back then. And what did you do in Dushanbe?'

'Worked with the Tajik Security Services. They were building up relations with Rabbani and Massood.'

'But why did you want to do all that? What was in it for you?'

'I am an employee. I follow my employer's orders. Just like you gentlemen do.' That was a lie, but the balaclava-clad men let it pass. They were employees too, but sure as hell, they were not following their employer's orders.

'And what was in it for your employer?' queried Tony.

'Like all other regional powers, India likes to be in control of its neighbourhood. Also, India has trouble in Kashmir and thinks that a friendly government in Afghanistan will make things easier.'

'Do you think India is justified in holding on to Kashmir?'

'I have just defected to your side. You gentlemen know why I have defected. What would you have me say? That India's stand is unjustified? That I think Pakistan is entitled to Kashmir? Would you believe me if I said that?' I bristled with anger.

'And what made you defect to us?' Rony asked me.

I was silent.

'Cat got your tongue?'

If the cat had bitten off my tongue, I wouldn't be able to reply, would I? I remained silent.

'I'll tell you why you defected. You defected because General West, your boss, had found out that you have been dipping your dirty kafir fingers into the till. You have been using for yourself money meant to be spent on informers. Like a dirty kafir, you have been drinking and gambling, all of this using office funds. You were about to be fired and maybe even put in jail, your past record be damned.'

I smiled. Not a smirking smile, but a tired smile that would not prick the ego of any of my tormentors sitting around the table. Ayub had an apologetic smile on his face, as if he was sorry I had to go through this, but that in any event, it was all for my own good.

'You are in such shit that you could not even defect to Faisal's side.' Faisal Yusuf was the ISI's UK head and he outranked every other ISI officer in the rest of Europe. In all probability, every one of those questioning me directly reported to Faisal Yusuf.

I couldn't take that stupid statement lying down. 'I don't agree,' I protested. 'Yes, if I had defected to the, to the…' I was going to say 'mainstream ISI', then I changed my mind and said, 'to Faisal Yusuf's side, they would have handed me back to General West, pronto. But that has nothing to do with my being in shit. Even if I weren't in shit, even if I was the IAG's model agent for the month or for the last ten months running, Faisal Yusuf would still have handed me back to the Intelligence Assessment Group (IAG). Gentlemen, it is true that I did not defect to your side for ideological reasons. I did it because I have nowhere else to go. However, we have a deal and I expect you to abide by that.' I tried to keep my voice polite, but firm.

That silenced them for the moment, but I knew that my respite wouldn't last for long. They hated me, hated what I had achieved in the past. They hated having to deal with me, a kafir who got into trouble because of excessive drinking and gambling.

'Did you ever visit Kabul when it was under Rabbani?'

'Yes, once. In 1995. I was there for a couple of weeks.'

'Where did you stay?' This was something they didn't know. I told them. It didn't matter. The dilapidated two-storeyed house I had sheltered in, disguised in a Pathan suit and turban, had been blown to bits by Gulbuddin Hekmatyar's artillery as he tried to take Kabul from the Northern Alliance. The people who had sheltered me, Hazaras eking out a bare living on the streets of Kabul, had long since disappeared.

'Did you meet with Najib?'

'Yes, I did.'

'And what did he have to say?'

'How does it matter?' I asked them warily.

'Tell us.' This time, Tony's probing was gentle, but persistent.

'He wanted to get out, to join his wife and children in Delhi. We were trying to persuade President Rabbani to let him go. We weren't successful.'

'Did you try very hard to free him from that UN compound?'

'Not really. He only had sentimental value.' That pleased the men for some reason and they all burst out laughing.

'We got to him, didn't we? He survived for four years in that compound, but we got to him in the end.'

Did it make each of you gents feel more of a man when the Talibs captured Najib, castrated him, stuffed his genitals into his mouth, beat him up and hanged him? I wanted to ask them.

'What did you do after we chased the Northern Alliance out of Kabul?'

'Nothing much. I continued in Dushanbe until 1998. Then I was sent to Almaty.'

'For how long were you in Almaty?'

'Until 9/11.' I hid my developing grin. That had been one of the biggest disasters from Pakistan's point of view. If only 9/11 hadn't taken place, the West wouldn't have given two hoots about the Taliban and the Pakistanis could have continued to use the Talibs to fight in Kashmir. 9/11 had messed up things for them, caused them so much trouble, anguish and dissension.

'You were seconded to General West's team after 9/11?' It was actually more of a statement than a question. They knew this to be a fact.

'Yes, immediately after 9/11, I was lent to the US and put in the IAG.'

'Is that when you moved to London?'

'Sort of. Initially I spent more time in Afghanistan than in London, but after I started to spend more time in London, I officially moved to London.' They didn't laugh at that, though I said 'moved' with an inflection. This was the sort of thing a Brit would have immediately laughed at. 'Of late, I've been spending almost all my time here, mainly doing paperwork. These chaps are so bureaucratic that—'

'These days you have been getting drunk in London, if I may say so.' There was a pause. 'General West heads the IAG, doesn't he?'

'Yes.' Were they happy with my brief response? Did they want me to tell them what I thought about General West? I don't know.

'How many in this group?'

'Around fifty.'

'And what does the IAG do?'

This was the easy part, the bit I knew by rote. 'The IAG is responsible for assessing intelligence gathered from Afghanistan by various coalition members. The intelligence gathered is pooled and assessed by the IAG here in London. Sometimes, they send people like me – men with experience – to Afghanistan. It doesn't matter which side we got that experience from – we are all based in London – but some of us go to Afghanistan to meet old contacts and collect intelligence.'

'He even has some Russians working for him, doesn't he? Your General West?'

'Yes, he does. But mainly Afghans and Pakistanis.' They didn't like that, but that was the truth so they couldn't do much about it.

'And what does that traitor, Rashid, do?'

'General Rashid Qayyum? Well, he is the senior-most among the Pakistanis in the IAG. He reports directly to General West like every other senior person.'

'You report directly to General West, don't you?'

'Yes, I do… I mean, I did.'

'So you are on par with General Qayyum?'

'Not exactly. He is a general. I am a civilian. I don't have a rank which can be compared with General Qayyum's. We are, or rather we were, pretty informal there. There is no strict hierarchy.'

'Did you ever have anything to do with Faisal Yusuf or Zahir Junejo?'

'I've met them both a few times. But no, I haven't worked with either of them much.'

'Yusuf works a lot with the IAG, doesn't he?'

'He does spend a lot of time with General West, but I have met him only a few times.'

'How many times have you met him?'

'Twice. Maybe thrice. I'm not sure.'

'Did you ever meet him alone?'

'No.'

'And what about Junejo?'

Ambassador Zahir Junejo's name was mentioned with a sneer; a tone of intense dislike and disrespect underlined every syllable of his name. This was in marked contrast to the way they referred to Faisal Yusuf whom they all evidently respected, though they didn't agree with his pro-US and anti-Taliban stance.

'He too spends a lot of time with General West. I have attended functions where he was present, but I have never met him on my own or worked on a project with him.'

'Do you think Junejo does any work? Don't you need to be sober to get some work done?'

I laughed aloud, but said nothing. There was no other way of handling the question. Zahir Junejo was a very intelligent man who enjoyed a tipple and made friends very easily. He was one of the best ambassadors Pakistan ever had. I have heard the Indian foreign secretary say aloud that he wished he could hire Ambassador Junejo and have him tutor his diplomats. However, for the pro-Taliban elements in the ISI and the Pakistani Foreign Service, Pakistan's ambassador to the Court of St. James was the very devil incarnate. It was not just his drinking and socialising that they objected to. Many of the pro-Taliban elements in the ISI and the Pakistani Foreign Service did the same. Unlike Faisal Yusuf who worked with the West mainly because he thought it was in Pakistan's interest to do so, Ambassador Junejo not only got along so well with the West, he was a genuine western aficionado. And that really got the pro-Taliban ISI's goat.

'I want you to write down the names of all the people you met and all that you did after you started working for General West.'

'Fine. I'll do that.'

A notebook and pen were placed in front of me. 'Shall I start?' I asked and indicated the notebook.

As if on cue, Rony launched into a verbal outburst, 'You ought to be ashamed of yourself, working for the Americans! Have they ever helped anyone in any part of the world?' I could almost see his moustache bristle under his balaclava.

I kept quiet as the four hooded men stared at me. Ayub was looking at his finger nails. I opened the notebook, uncapped the pen and started writing, upon which the four men got up and walked out. Ayub gave the men a cheerful smile as they filed out.

'I have something for you, gentlemen, before you leave.' The men stopped in their tracks.

I took out a piece of paper from the pocket of my trousers. 'This has details of two drone attacks that will be carried out in Waziristan and Helmand sometime tomorrow, early morning local time. You could pass this on to the people who could do something about it.'

Ayub whistled. The sheet of paper had a small hand-drawn map on each side with something jotted down in Persian.

'Who prepared this map? Who's writing is it?'

'It's mine. These attacks were planned late last night. I played a small role in choosing these targets. One of my contacts gave me a tip for the Helmand target. The one in Waziristan was picked on the basis of intelligence collected by one of General West's aides.'

'Thank you very much, Ritwik.' Rony sounded genuinely grateful. 'We'll make sure that the Infidels don't harm the Faithful with these attacks. Now you start writing down details of all your contacts in Afghanistan. Make sure you write down the name of the bastard in Helmand who told you about this target.'

'Sure. Can I use the loo before I start?' I asked Ayub.

'Of course.'

I went to the toilet and found it shut. I waited outside the door impatiently for a few minutes until it opened and a man I had never seen before came out, twirling a car key in his hand. The fifth man among those five men who had come to meet me was now accounted for. I happily went inside and relieved myself.

# 4

THERE WAS A LOUD BANGING on the door. I woke up and looked at the luminous face of my watch. It was a quarter past one in the morning. Wearily, I got out of bed.

◇

The room they had given me for the night was as Spartan as the room in which I had been debriefed. Apart from a single iron bedstead, a lumpy mattress, a not-so-thick duvet and a portable heater that barely kept the room warm, there was nothing else. The bedstead's headstand consisted of a series of parallel vertical bars with a five-inch gap between two bars, which meant it was too uncomfortable to lean against. A small duffel bag on the floor contained the few clothes and toiletries that Junaid had got for me. I now had two toothbrushes! Since my old toothbrush had bristles spread out like a cauliflower, I planned to use the new one. My jacket hung on one of the bedposts. The room had a large window, about five feet high and eight feet wide, the base of which was just above my knees, but it was boarded up. The loo was equally bare. It had a few rolls of toilet paper and a can of liquid soap, but no mirror. The lack of a mirror reminded me of a prison. If Ayub was around I would have demanded that they give me something better. However, Ayub was nowhere to be seen. Before I was shown to my room, Ayub had collected the notebook in which I had written down names and other details of people I had worked with in Afghanistan, and disappeared.

After dinner with Junaid that was as tasty as the earlier lunch, I went to bed at eight-thirty. I was tired and there was nothing else to do. There was no television in the house and Junaid wasn't exactly a conversationalist. In fact, he hardly spoke a word. The man seemed to be perfectly content sitting right across me on the sofa, wrapped up in a silence where even thoughts didn't seem to intrude. The living room had a window but the curtains were drawn. There were potted plants by the window-sill and these were actually kept on top of the curtain ends so that even an accidental breeze wouldn't cause the curtains to move. It was intentional, I was sure. My hosts didn't want me looking out of any window and shouting out to a passerby.

That evening, Junaid disappeared for short intervals at least five times, of which two were for prayers. The low monotone in Arabic that emanated from the adjacent room was definitely in keeping with Junaid's appearance. The only exciting part of the evening had been when a woman, covered from head to toe in a black burkha, walked lithely into the room, opened a cupboard, took something out and walked out again. She was short and to all appearances, very plump. Her small, bright, round eyes were the only visible parts of her body, and they avoided mine altogether. Was it because she hated me, a kafir or because she was expected not to make eye contact with a strange man? After she left, I had asked Junaid, 'Is that your wife?' I had got a nod in response. It was obvious that Junaid didn't like to discuss his wife, much less introduce her to me. Well, I had no grievances on that score. I wasn't there to make friends with the women in the household.

✧

I drew myself out of my reverie. The banging had become louder. I quickly walked towards the door. It sounded as if the impatient men on the other side of the door would tear it down any moment. As soon as I opened the door, a light was shone onto my face and a bunch of men rushed into the room. Instinctively my hand went inside my jacket, except that I was dressed in a pair of striped pyjamas, which looked as if they had been acquired from a charity shop, and in any event didn't allow for a firearm to be tucked inside. Not that I had one at that moment. By this time, two men had me by each arm and another had my neck in an arm lock. Having wasted precious seconds trying to draw a non-existent weapon, I swung my right leg randomly at the man standing to my left. I was lucky and heard a very satisfactory cracking sound as my heel made contact with a kneecap. The man went down with a grunt and fell down with a thump.

At this, the rest of the men started to rain blows on me. The arm around my neck tightened substantially causing a sudden drop in the flow of oxygen to my head. I gave up and went limp. The men dragged me to my bed. I wished they would switch on the light and stop shining the headlamp onto my face. They didn't. However, the pressure on my neck eased after a few more moments.

'We found out about you!' I was told in Urdu.

'Found out what?' I managed to splutter.

'That you are a double agent!'

'Like hell I am!' That retort earned me a punch on my abdomen that narrowly missed my solar plexus. It hurt nevertheless.

'You thought you would get away with it, didn't you?' Someone asked me. I tried to focus on the voices around me. Ayub didn't seem to be among the men holding me. One of the men standing nearby seemed to be Junaid. There couldn't be too many men with a frame and build so similar. I was slapped across my face twice by a man in a balaclava. Someone switched off the heater.

'Admit it, you are a double-crosser,' I was told once more.

'Listen, there's a terrible mistake somewhere. I am genuine. Twenty-four carat.'

A chair was brought into the room and I was made to sit on it. My hands were tied behind me, with the arms of the chair between my trussed up hands and my back.

'You won't suffer if you confess,' another voice announced before a bucket of cold water was dumped on me.

As I shivered, the strings of my pyjamas were undone. The moment the clip was fastened to my dick, I started to scream. 'You bastards are totally mistaken. Ayub, where the fuck are you?'

'You dirty, double-crossing bastard, you thought you could take us for a ride, didn't you? You'll tell us the truth when we light you up.'

'Stop this right away!' It was Ayub's firm voice. He made his way towards me through the melee. 'Someone switch on the light.'

The men, reluctantly, made way for him. The beam being shone on my face was turned off and the light in the room was switched on. Ayub had a pained look on his face. There were around ten men in the room, of which five wore balaclavas. I was right about Junaid. He stood in a corner, looking highly irritated, most probably because of disturbed sleep than me being a double-crosser.

'Ritwik, you've got me into this shit as well. We've found out that you are a double-agent. The whole thing is a sham, isn't it?' Ayub asked, his voice showing a mix of anger, sadness and bewilderment.

'Of course not! Why on earth would you say that?' I asked Ayub angrily.

'You tell me that! One of our agents in Delhi has reported that you are a double agent. This source has never been wrong. We have no choice but to believe that chap.'

'Listen, somebody has made a terrible mistake. If only you would present the evidence against me, I can–'

'Yeah, that's how we operate, right? By presenting evidence and giving everyone a chance to defend themselves. Why don't you admit your guilt and save yourself a lot of pain?'

'What about the information I gave you? The drone attack must have taken place by now.'

'Yes, both attacks, just as you predicted. In Helmand and Waziristan. Thanks to the information you gave us, we were able to move our people out in time. But that doesn't prove anything, Ritwik. You know that. If you are a double agent, you'd be easily able to arrange for a couple of drone attacks.'

Ayub moved back and two of the men came forward. I could see that the wire attached to me led to a car battery kept on a wheelbarrow, the common sort that's used in gardens.

'Go on, do it,' a man in a balaclava ordered in a stern voice.

'For god's sake, I am no double agent! If you use that thing on me for long, I am bound to confess. Everyone does.'

'You'll also have to tell us why you are here, what you are hoping to achieve, why you went through the charade of pretending to be a drunkard and a gambler. You'll have to tell us all that. And it should all add up. Else you will suffer a lot.'

That voice sounded very familiar, but neither was it Ayub's nor Junaid's. I tried to focus on the source of the voice, something not so easy since my entire face was stinging from the slaps I had received. Munir had a messianic look on his face, instead of his usual absentminded one.

'I can't tell you all that, but I am not a miserable double-agent.' I was genuinely scared and I guess the fear was conveyed in my voice.

'Tell you what, we'll give you the whole night,' Ayub chipped in. 'We'll come back at six in the morning and you make up your mind by then. If you confess by then, well and good. If not, I'll have no choice but to step aside and let these men do what they were planning to do now.'

Even as I bellowed, 'It won't make any bloody difference,' they untied me and unclipped the electrodes.

'Take his watch,' said Munir. 'The light.'

Someone took off my watch, just as the light was turned off. A patter of feet marched out of the room.

'The toilet's locked. If you need to relieve yourself, you'll have to do it in a corner.'

The door slammed shut, and I was alone once again. I sat on the chair shivering. My whole body was wet, the floor was wet and it was cold as hell. I got up gingerly, retied my pyjama strings and walked towards the door so that I could switch on the light. The clicking sound was unaccompanied by the expected brightness. Bastards! Someone had unscrewed the bulb and taken it away as they walked out. Munir had said 'The light', but I didn't expect them to have removed the bulb. Never mind, I told myself. I still had a small pocket torch inside my jacket. I walked over to the bed and groped for my jacket. I couldn't find it. Had I stuffed it into the duffel bag along with my clothes and toiletries? The duffel bag wasn't where it had been earlier. I groped in the darkness and found nothing. My shoes ought to have been under the bed, but they weren't there either. The portable heater. Was it still there? No, it had been taken away as well.

My heart was beating fast. Sit down and relax, I told myself. This was only expected. I realised that I was squatting on the floor. I slowly crawled back to the bed so that I could dry myself between the mattress and the duvet, using one side and later, snuggle into the other side. My fingers rested on the cold frame of the iron bedstead. The bed was bare and the mattress and duvet were missing.

It took me a few minutes to regain my composure. I got up and walked over to the toilet. Damn! It *was* locked. I considered kicking open the door, but remembered that the door opened outwards. Unless I actually broke the door, which wouldn't be easy since I was barefooted, I wouldn't be able to open it.

I went back to the bed and sat down. The cold iron bit into my bum. I stretched myself out and tried to sleep, but I was so nervous and scared that I couldn't. What were they getting at, I wondered. A confession extracted under torture was worth nothing, everyone knew. Actually that was poppycock. A confession prised out using force, was worth a lot, if it synched with other available information. If a thief confesses his theft after having the living daylights beaten out of him, the confession as such is worthless. However, if his confession leads to the stolen property, which might still have his prints on them, there is a very good chance of securing a conviction.

Why do they want me to confess, I wondered. Either they trusted me or they didn't. Maybe their source in Delhi wasn't as confident as they had made it sound. Maybe it was not as trusted a source as they had made it out to be. If the pro-Taliban ISI believed that I was a double agent, the best thing I could hope for was a speedy death, though I was much more likely to receive a painful one and disposal in a container of concrete somewhere in the Thames. I told myself that if I had any sense, I would slash my wrists or something and make the rest of my life relatively comfortable, while I still could.

I was desperate to pee. Hold on till six, I told myself. If I hadn't been woken up and made to undergo the special treatment I had just received, I wouldn't have wanted to use the toilet till I woke up in the morning, would I? However, some allowance had to be made for the bucket of cold water poured on me and being in a room with no heating. The men had entered the room at quarter past one. It was bound to be around two-thirty now. Another three-and-a-half hours and they would come for me again.

I took off my wet pyjama top, wrung it, wiped myself with it and put it back on. I felt better and stopped shivering for a while, but a few minutes later, I started to shiver yet again. It was bitterly cold. I started to repeat the names of all those who were at the Civil Services Academy at Mussoorie with me to veer my mind and body away from the cold. Then I went on to all my colleagues when I was at the embassy in Moscow. My classmates at my Russian language class. Dushanbe followed. And then, Kabul. All the informers I had recruited. All the double agents I had discovered and despatched. I had been in too many places, tried my hand at more than a few languages, met too many people and made very few friends.

Far too few, but they were tried and tested though, even if none of them could help me at this moment.

I needed to pee pretty badly now. Was it almost six? There was no way I would know. What time was sunrise? It was January. Winter. What time was sunrise? Six-thirty? No, maybe seven. Was that a chink of light that shone through a hole in the window boarding? No, it was just a speck of white on the boarding. My eyes had almost deceived me. The window had been boarded up tightly. The toilet door was shut firmly. Too tightly. Too firmly. They had prepared for my arrival. It looked as if they had made all these preparations so that they could threaten me and beat me. Why then didn't they put me through the wringer as soon as I arrived? Why did they wait till I had settled in and fallen asleep? I started to smile, despite my chattering teeth. I wondered whose idea this was. It didn't sound like Ayub. It couldn't be Junaid. That man's brain would be worth a lot of money after he died. It would be almost entirely unused. As good as new. Most probably it was Munir. Munir, the genius. The intellectual. I grimly promised myself that one day I would pay him back in the same coin

I went to a corner and relieved myself. The stench rose to the air. To use a pun I have found scrawled above many urinals, I shook myself well after use, pulled up my pyjamas and went to sleep on the iron bedstead. I continued to shiver as the smell of urine filled up the room. Sleep eluded me for another hour, after which my weariness triumphed over the cold and discomfort.

# 5

JUNAID OPENED THE DOOR AND let Munir and five other men in along with some light from the living room. Except for Munir and Junaid, everyone else looked as menacing as before with their faces covered. The Pakistani embassy was most probably working at half strength that day, with a notice apologising to visitors for being short-staffed. '*We apologise for any inconvenience caused due to short staffing. Please note that half our employees have fallen mysteriously ill and will continue to be ill until the Ritwik Kumar affair is sorted out.*' Munir had a grim expression on his face. Everyone else wrinkled their noses since the whole room stank like a cesspool.

'We have been given irrefutable proof that you're a double-agent. Rather than torture you, we've decided that it's best for everyone if you're sent off to meet your maker. Do you have anything to say?'

I worked hard at looking scared. 'Listen, you got it all wrong. I can explain everything. I am not a double-agent. I, I—'

'Kneel.' The peremptory order stopped me from explaining any further.

I hesitated. Junaid came over and roughly forced me to the ground. Instead of kneeling, I squatted. One of the hooded men drew out a pistol, an old fashioned Colt with many scratches on it, and pointed it at my head. After a few seconds of that, Junaid took out a towel from his jacket and blindfolded me.

'This is how we deal with double-agents,' Munir bellowed. 'For the last time, do you want to confess?'

'For the last time, NO. And for the record, you are an arsehole!' It crossed my mind that I had miscalculated and that my brains might be blown to smithereens at any moment. I felt an irresistible impulse to confess, to scream 'Don't shoot, I am a double agent!' I kept my mouth shut, thought my knees almost buckled. They had promised to come for me at six in the morning, but somehow I knew that it was way past six. If their objective was to make me disoriented, they had been successful. I had lost all sense of time. I waited and waited. Time seemed to stand still.

After a minute, my blindfold was taken off, and Munir hugged me. 'Ritwik, you are one of us now,' he said and immediately drew back. I had pissed inside that room twice that night. The whole room stank like an unkempt urinal and I doubt if I smelt any different.

'What's happening?' I asked in puzzlement and wonder at my new lease of life.

'It was only a test. And you passed with flying colours. You are one of us.'

'What time is it?' I asked after the shock and surprise subsidised.

'Three p.m. You must be hungry.'

So it was three p.m. No wonder I was so exhausted. 'Thirsty and hungry. But I need a bath first.'

As I ate my lunch, lamb biryani this time, I could hear some sweeping and scrubbing sounds from my bedroom. It was being cleaned. I wondered if Junaid was upset with the way his house was being misused. If he was, he didn't show it. His face remained as impassive as ever.

The curtains still covered the windows in the living room and the potted plants were in their usual places on top of the curtain ends.

'Do you mind drawing the curtain?' I asked Ayub.

'If you don't mind, old chap, we have our instructions. This won't be for more than a few days, I assure you.'

'And I thought at least now we are on the same side.' I shook my head in disbelief.

Ayub shrugged, as if to say, rules are rules and there was nothing much he could do about them.

When I had finished lunch, Ayub came in. There were a few flakes of snow on his head.

'Snowing outside?'

'Yes. It's been snowing since early morning and pretty heavily too. This cold snap is going to last for a bit. I'm glad you got here yesterday rather than today. The tube isn't operational on most lines. Most train companies are offering a limited service. Even the scheduled trains are all delayed. There are so many stranded vehicles on the roads that—'

'Was it your idea?'

Ayub grimaced and shook his head. Munir looked uncomfortable. 'This is a test that never fails. You won't believe how many double-agents we have uncovered by this …' Munir hesitated a bit before saying 'by this tactic'.

Munir fascinated me as much as Junaid. Just like Junaid, he was also British born and bred, with a local accent to boot. Unlike Ayub who was very British though not British born, Munir looked and played the part of an Islamic ideologue. If I had been told that he had just arrived in the UK a few weeks ago, I would have believed it, save for his accent, which was part Cockney and part BBC. His paunch bespoke one who shirked any form of physical activity. I wasn't sure where he fitted into the hierarchy within the pro-Taliban ISI in London. It was obvious that Ayub and other Pakistanis called the shots over locally bred boys like Junaid and Munir. Did Munir have a large following within the fundamentalist fringe in London? Could he, with a single phone call, muster a mob who would unleash mayhem? Could he be a preacher in a mosque who, with his oration, could incite men to jihad? Or was he just a paper tiger Ayub used to run his errands? He couldn't be just an errand boy; he had persuaded Ayub to put me to the test. However, I just couldn't imagine him calling the shots. The jigsaw puzzle had a piece missing, one that I'd have to locate if I were to survive.

'The Foreign Office has put out a general alert for you.' Ayub announced as he sat on the sofa.

'Is it official?' I asked.

'Yes. The hunt for you is officially on since this morning. MI5 and MI6 have circulated your details to all their people. The IAG has sent memos to all friendly intelligence agencies. The high commission has received one. We had a laugh when we got the fax. Your photo doesn't do much justice to you.' Ayub laughed at the recollection.

'There's one file photo they have which is particularly ghastly. I have a pretty nasty crew cut and it's over five years old. Is that the—'

'Yes, that sounds like the one they've used. I wonder why they do that. The Met police have been asked to keep an eye out for you. Your house has been raided and sealed. When I drove past this morning, they had put up yellow tape all around and I could see a police car parked outside.'

'It was a nice house,' I sighed.

'Your friends Bob and Eddie will be in for a surprise if they decide to pay you another visit.'

'If only you guys had paid me the money I asked for, I could have paid those guys off, put back the money I had used up and carried on as usual and given you chaps a lot more information than you'll get from me now.'

'My dear man, you wanted us to pay you five million dollars. I doubt if you would have got that kind of money even if you were defecting to Faisal's side. I still can't understand how you managed to steal so much and lose it all on horses.'

Munir burst out saying, 'Faisal might have paid you five million, but he would've immediately told the Yankees that you are a traitor to your own people and demanded ten million dollars from the Americans as a reward for having done his two bit for peace in the subcontinent.'

I turned to Ayub for confirmation. After all, Faisal was Ayub's boss. I wondered if Faisal suspected Ayub. In all likelihood he didn't. Ayub was so anglicised and so much of a public school boy that it was difficult to imagine him with his Oxbridge accent sympathising with Islamic fundamentalists, much less working for them. 'Is that true? Is Faisal the sort of man who'll give me money so that I can bail myself out and then snitch to the Americans that I have sold myself out?'

'Well, I can't imagine Faisal paying you any money while you are in the IAG. If you had approached him, he might have humoured you for a bit, while he passed on the information to the Americans. You obviously know that. Else you would have approached Faisal. He's not a bad man. He's just like anyone else in this profession. He doesn't mind dirty tricks if the potential returns justify it. He believes Pakistan is better off without the Taliban. I respectfully disagree with him. I think we need the Taliban as our allies if we are to survive as a nation. Pakistan should go back to the pre-9/11 era. The time when the Taliban controlled Afghanistan and helped us in Kashmir and elsewhere.'

'You think the Taliban will be happy with just Afghanistan if they are to win this round and get the Americans to leave. Won't they want to control Pakistan as well? Isn't the Taliban already fighting for control of Pakistan? Haven't so many

Pakistani soldiers died fighting the Taliban in Swat and Waziristan and elsewhere?'

'Control is a word with variable meaning. We rubbed them the wrong way and some sections of the Talibs are fighting us at home. They are fighting us because we support the Yanks in Afghanistan. The Taliban are entitled to share power in Pakistan. There is nothing wrong in sharing power with them. But they won't be the sole decision-makers. Once Afghanistan reverts to their control and the Americans leave, Pakistan and the Taliban will stop fighting each other. We'll go back to when the frontier was quiet.'

'Do you agree with that?' I turned to Munir who didn't look very convinced.

'We want the whole world to be under our control. Of course, the people will have the right to decide for themselves how to live. But it will be an Islamic world. I just—'

Ayub didn't let Munir complete. He turned to me and said, 'You still haven't really told us how you managed to lose five million in just six months.' It was a bit obvious that he wanted to cross examine me rather than allow me to quiz him on his ideology.

'It wasn't just horses. There was some spread betting, lottery tickets, stocks and bonds, some plain vanilla, some complicated derivatives…'

'I know, I know, you've told me all that, but….'

'Of course, drinking liquor costs money. The man who supplied me with Old Monk, he used to charge me a fortune for that stuff. You can't get that here, you need to import it.'

'Why do you have to drink Old Monk? It isn't anything great. It's not as if you don't get decent liquor in London.'

'I know, but I'm just too used to it and nothing else can really substitute Old Monk.'

'That still doesn't explain how you managed to get through so much—'

'It's unbelievable how much it costs to have a good time in the West End.'

Munir was looking at me with the sort of fascination usually reserved for the devil. As for Junaid, his face remained as impassive as ever.

'What did you do with my Blackberry?' I asked Ayub.

'It's in the Thames now. Broken and crushed. Crushed to the extent a Blackberry can be. They make those instruments bloody sturdy. I wonder if the tracking device inside will work under water?'

'Yes it will. The Foreign Office is capable of locating a Blackberry even if its owner drowns. Or is drowned.'

'I did the best I could.'

'My dear Ayub, you should have had it burnt. Didn't you think of it?'

'No, why didn't you tell me?'

'I thought you'd think of it.'

'Never mind.'

'Listen, all those contacts you wrote down in that notebook, they are—'

'I wrote down the details of everyone I have worked with in Afghanistan since 1987.'

'Many of them are a bit outdated.'

'I know they are. But not all of them.'

'No? Well, we are yet to work our way through all the names.'

Junaid's burkha-clad wife entered the room to clear the plates that were still on the table. As she gathered up the plates and walked out, my leg stretched out a little further than it had any right to be. The woman went flying, along with her plates. As she fell down, the lower end of the burkha flew up revealing a trouser leg that ended in a very cheap blue sock, stuffed into a plain black shoe. But not for long. Junaid quickly pulled the woman to her feet and ushered her away, leaving the plates on the floor. I bent down and started to pick up the plates. Munir joined me, but not before I had three plates and two bowls in my hand. Even as a surprised Munir got up with a plate and two spoons in his hand, I quickly followed Junaid to the kitchen. I didn't go in, but stood outside, my face displaying the timidity that goes so well on a visitor's face inside a traditional South Asian household.

The sound of a slap was all too audible to me as I stood outside the kitchen, Munir stood just behind me. 'Why can't you be more careful, you bitch?' Junaid asked his wife in the best Cockney accent in the world. He then switched to Punjabi and added something that I didn't quite catch. It's not that my Punjabi isn't fluent, though I subscribe to the eastern version and Junaid was speaking in the western one spoken in Pakistan. Junaid spoke Punjabi with such a heavy English accent that it was tough to understand what he was saying. I heard sobs and a few seconds later, Junaid came out. He was surprised to see me standing outside the door, but before he could say anything, I pressed the plates into his hands and retreated. Munir followed me.

As I went back to the sofa, Munir came up to me and

said, 'Junaid is a good guy, but sometimes he gets carried away. Islam doesn't advocate this sort of stuff, you know.'

I shrugged my shoulders. It was none of my business. I was a gambler and a drunkard who had been forced to defect to a side that hated people like me more than they hated anyone else. I shrugged my shoulders again as I wanted to tell Ayub and Munir that it was none of my business. Ayub looked at us with curiosity, but didn't say anything. I wondered what was going on in his mind. Maybe he just wanted the whole chapter to be over as quickly as possible.

Soon Junaid was back. 'All well?' Munir asked him.

'Yes.'

He looked at me with hatred, as if I were a cockroach, something he could stamp on and finish in a jiffy. However, he was a loyal soldier and within seconds, his impassive face was back on. I was safe for the moment.

Exhaustion soon hit me hard. I yawned desperately and stretched myself. After a while Ayub was forced to say, 'Maybe you should take a nap. You wouldn't have got much sleep last night.' He hid his smile.

I looked at my watch again. It was five o'clock. I looked at the large clock on the wall for confirmation.

'Maybe you could nap for a couple of hours. You can get up before dinner.'

I was shown to my room, the same one where I had been locked up until a few hours ago. However, it now smelt of a cheap air freshener and the window boarding had been taken off. It was dark outside but I could see that my room overlooked a yard which had a grassy patch, a few shrubs and what looked like an apple tree. I wished the large window had curtains. The idea that anyone could look inside my room from the garden made me uncomfortable, but there was nothing I could do about it. I looked around the room casually as I changed into the new pair of pyjamas that I found in my duffel bag. If there was a camera inside the room, it was hidden well. The wires around the window were a different matter altogether. They undoubtedly connected to a burglar alarm, but more importantly, they were not concealed, more so to send out a clear message to me. Do not open the window. I switched off the light and went to the loo.

The toilet roll holder was one of those hollow steel pipes screwed into a cylindrical base. I took out the toilet paper, unscrewed the steel pipe and kept it under my shirt. I went back to the dark bedroom and got into bed. Eyes closed, I started to breathe heavily, almost snore, within a few minutes. After a decent interval, by which time whosoever was watching or listening was hopefully bored and would have given up, I slowly turned around under the duvet, but continued to breathe heavily. Silently, I pulled out the hollow steel pipe from under my shirt. I held one end of it to the wall, under the cover of the duvet, and listened through the other end, my left ear pressed into the hollow. I kept listening for a while. After some time I could hear sounds of sobbing. The sobs grew into wails. In the next few minutes, I could hear the wails without the steel pipe, which I put away. I wished I could talk to that woman and console her. Instead, I went back to the toilet and replaced the steel pipe. Back on my bed, I soon drifted off to sleep.

# 6

'TELL ME ABOUT KARIM,' AYUB prodded me. 'He's the only one who's of interest to us.'

'For the last six months, I haven't really done much work on my contacts. I ought to have, but I didn't and that's what got me into this predicament.'

'Well, it's a good thing you bargained hard and refused to give us your contacts until you came over. If you had shown us this list before your defection, I might have been forced to ask you to stay where you are. You would have been rotting inside a British jail by now.'

'Ayub, you're being too harsh on me. Surely as my case officer, it's in your interest as well to show your friends that I am valuable? What'll they think of you if you go to them and say that I haven't brought over anything of interest?'

'Unfortunately your notes have been pored over by all those who interrogated you yesterday. It's a joint verdict that you haven't brought over much that's useful.'

'There's Karim, there's Jabbar, there's—'

'Tell me about Karim.'

'He's roughly my age. In his late forties. Looks much older. Lives in a village on the outskirts of the town of Kajaki in the Helmand province. He's a Pashtun. His family fought the Soviets. After 1989, Karim was in Hekmatyar's militia. Later he went over to the Taliban. One of your blue-eyed boys. I'm sure your friends in Pakistan have records of him. Mullah Omar has stayed at his place a few times. Currently, he tills a few acres of land on which he grows poppies. The Talibs buy his harvest each year at a decent price.'

'And he's going to switch sides?'

'Well, sort of. Karim had a son, a fourteen-year-old boy – the apple of his eye. He has three daughters as well, but this son was his youngest child and meant everything to him. Last year Karim sent off his fourteen-year-old son to fight full-time for the Taliban.'

'Actually I know all this, Ritwik. The son's dead, isn't he? Get to the point, will you? Your notes were very cryptic. All they say is Karim, farmer in Kajaki, Helmand, going to switch sides. Will help capture Talib leaders who stay there from time to time.'

'Let me get to it, will you? Last year there was an accident. While on patrol, Karim's son stepped on a landmine and died. I managed to persuade Karim that his son was actually killed by one of the big men he was with, who is known to be fond of young boys. Told him that his young son had resisted an advance and had been killed as a punishment and as a warning to other boys. Because this big man has a good reputation, Karim believed me and has promised to switch sides.'

'Just like that? You told him this and he believed you? When did you talk to Karim?'

'I've had three meetings with him. The first was a few weeks after the boy died. I took along with me a man who told Karim he was a witness to his son being choked to death.'

'This man…was he a defector?'

'Yes, he was switching sides. He is now somewhere in the north. In a safe place.'

'You met Karim again, after that?'

'Twice. The second time was a few months later. Karim promised to think it over, my proposal that is. He was still grief-stricken. The third time was just over a month ago. That's when he was planning to switch. I told him to stay on till a few big men come visiting. We'd drop in, pick them up in a way that wouldn't compromise Karim.'

'Now that you are with us, I guess we can kill Karim, can't we?'

'Yes, you could. Else, if you like, I could go and meet him and tell him that it was all a story. He might believe me.'

'Even if he does, I doubt if he will be forgiven. Karim will have to go.'

'Pity.'

'But that's something useful you've told us.'

'I could tell him that it was all a farce, that his son was killed thanks to the landmine.'

'You don't get it, do you? The Afghans don't work like that. Karim agreed to betray his masters and he must pay for it. That Karim was tricked into such a position doesn't make any difference. Betrayal is nothing but that, irrespective of the background or the motive. Surely you know that better than most other people.'

I sighed and said, 'Yes I do. But if there were to be a direct order that Karim be preserved, won't that happen?'

'We don't really control the Taliban. They can't be controlled in matters like this. I've passed on this info. Let's see what happens.'

I dropped Karim. There was no point flogging a dead horse. 'Forget Karim then. If you send me back to Afghanistan, I can go and meet my old contacts, persuade them to come to your side. You can send someone along with me, with the money, I don't trust myself with money any more. But I can give something back to you. You'll get something out of me.'

'So you want to go back to Afghanistan?'

'I've always said that, haven't I? Right from the time you and Junaid saved me from Bob and Eddie and took me to that pub. I need to be in a place where I can't get access to liquor or the casino.'

Ayub laughed at that. 'No worries. Now that you are with us, we won't let you drink yourself to death.'

We were silent for a while. Then I asked Ayub, 'Do you think you can give me one of my Old Monk bottles? I'd like to have a drink. Never been without a drink for so long. I think I'm having withdrawal symptoms.'

'No,' said Junaid before Ayub could react. This was my third day as a defector. We were sitting in Junaid's living room, having finished breakfast a short while ago. Munir wasn't around. By now, I'd come to think of Junaid as a fixture, a piece of furniture. I hadn't seen his wife after that tripping incident. If Junaid still harboured any ill-will towards me on account of that, he was hiding it very well.

'Can't I have a drink in your garden? That's not your house,' I beseechingly asked Junaid.

'No. No.'

'Can I go to a pub nearby with one of you and get a drink? I'm dying for one.'

'Ritwik, I can't see any harm, but I don't have the permission to let you do that. I'll get into trouble,' Ayub was quick to say. It was hot water I knew, but I let it pass.

'Why don't you have someone drive me around in a car, while I have a quick one. I won't step out of the car.'

'Ritwik, don't do this to me. I just don't have the authority to let you go anywhere outside this house. It doesn't make a difference whether you actually set foot outside or not.'

'I'd like to go for a walk. No booze. Just a walk. Just fresh air.'

'I don't think it is a good idea, Ritwik,' spoke Ayub bluntly. 'It's actually for your own good.'

'Come off it, Ayub. You don't think I am going to feel guilty and go back to where I came from.'

'It's been known to happen.'

'Yes, but you know me.'

'I have my orders.' Again I knew that it was bullshit. If Ayub wanted to let me go for a walk, he could. Of course, if I jumped ship led a team of Metropolitan policemen to their safe-house, it would be Ayub's neck on the line.

'How long do you think it will be before you reach a decision regarding me?'

'Not too long I hope. We don't have much red tape. Everything is done on an informal basis.'

'Can I at least go for a prowl in the garden?'

'It's cold.'

'Can I?'

Ten minutes later, a disgruntled-looking Junaid and I were in the garden, both of us wrapped up to our ears against the bitter cold. The snow on the ground was a couple of inches high and some of it was fresh. The UK must be having a record snowfall this year, I thought. The wooden door, which led to the garden from the kitchen, was partly open and it creaked a bit as it swung to and fro in the wind, until Ayub or someone else closed it from inside. Leaving it open would have allowed those in the house to keep an eye on me, but that would let the cold inside. Not that there was a big security risk with Junaid near me, his eyes never wavering from me even for a millisecond.

I desperately wished I could listen to the weather report on the Beeb, even if they got it wrong more often than not. I wanted to read *The Times*, as I usually did every morning, whatever time I woke up. I clenched and unclenched my fists and the longing went away. From the garden, I could look into my pitiful bedroom, through its window. The place where I had suffered so much humiliation and degradation looked tiny from outside.

I walked over to the other end of the garden, which had an apple tree close to the corner. However, it was a smallish tree and I wouldn't have been able to use it to climb up the tall wooden fence that ringed the garden forming a sort of semi-circle. The sides of that damned fence conjoined the house, denying access to the courtyard in the front, unless of course one had a key to the big lock that hung on the small door on the right side of the garden that obviously led to the courtyard. Escape was impossible. Even if I were to open my bedroom window and enter the garden without setting off the burglar alarm, I would find it difficult to climb over the fence without a ladder. A few chrysanthemums and roses stood in a patch near the apple tree, all mixed up. The rest of the garden was unkempt – tall grass stood out at a few places in the snow. A bit like my own courtyard which never once saw a lawnmower while I lived there.

'How's your wife?' I asked Junaid. 'I hope she wasn't hurt when she fell down yesterday.'

I got a baleful look in response to my statement, which was actually a question. I decided not to repeat it. Instead, I told him, 'I have this brilliant idea. I wonder what Ayub will make of it when I tell him.'

'What's the idea?' Junaid was forced to ask, a mixture of forced politeness, impatience and curiosity on his face.

'If your wife was put in charge of this house and you took orders from her, things would be much better.'

It took a minute for my words to sink in. When they did, Junaid lunged at me, his enormous palms balled into fists. In his rage, he didn't take his woollen gloves off. I stepped aside and kicked him in his balls from the side. Junaid's actions were motivated by pure anger. Further, he was undoubtedly restrained by Ayub's orders to make sure that I was kept in fine fettle, preferably alive. I, on the other hand, was prepared to and wanted to cause grievous injury. I had the advantage of having anticipated Junaid's reaction. When Junaid bent down to clutch his crown jewels, I took my right glove off with my left hand and hit him on the back of his head using my right palm. For most men, a kick in the balls followed by a chop to the back of the head would be enough to knock them out cold. But not for Junaid. Ordinary rules didn't apply to him.

Within a second of receiving a blow to the back of his head, Junaid swung his left arm backwards in a vicious arc and caught me with a glancing blow to my left ribcage. I staggered back a few steps, stopped myself and then lunged forward to fall onto Junaid's back and tried to choke him from behind. That was another mistake. With a deep grunt, Junaid got up and threw me on the ground. If he had wanted, he could have turned around and killed me with a single kick. Instead, he sluggishly put his hand inside his jacket, trying to reach for his berretta. I picked up a large lump of snow and threw it at Junaid's face, blinding him temporarily. Junaid took his hand out of his jacket and wiped the snow off his face. Then again, he reached for something in his jacket. As I picked up the snow, my fingers brushed against something hard. It was a small piece of rock.

I knew this wasn't cricket, but I had a lot more to lose than any cricketer ever did. I took an aim at Junaid's forehead even as his berretta came out.

I didn't miss. It would have been stupid to miss at such close range. Junaid was knocked out cold. I was panting. Each breath I took hurt, which meant that one or more of my ribs were bruised, if not broken. I picked up my glove from the snow and slid my hand into it as I waited for my breathing to slow down. With considerable effort, I opened the door that led to the kitchen. I stuffed the berretta back inside Junaid's jacket. Lifting up Junaid by his armpits, I dragged him inside the house through the snow, dumped him on the floor and waited for Ayub to poke his head through the door and shoot me dead.

It was not Ayub, but Junaid's wife who made an appearance. She must have heard something heavy being dragged into the house for she walked into the kitchen hesitantly, her face fully covered in a burkha. On seeing Junaid lying on the floor, a big cut above his eye, she gasped.

'Don't worry,' I told her in Punjabi. 'Junaid slipped and hurt himself. He'll be okay in a while. Can you get some cold water? And where's Ayub?'

Instead of responding to my questions, she just stood there and gaped. I know that she gaped because her small, bright, round eyes almost bulged out of the black stuff that covered her from head to toe.

'Don't be afraid,' I repeated in Punjabi. Something in her eyes suggested that she understood what I was saying.

'Ayub-bhai left a while ago,' she spoke hesitantly.

'Can you please give Ayub a call and ask him to come back immediately? I'm sure you have his number.'

'No, I have nobody's number.' The lady showed no inclination to fetch water. Then she asked me in English, 'What really happened? Did you hit him?'

I was a bit surprised. I didn't expect the burkha-clad wife to speak English. It wasn't southern standard English which the BBC followed, but the subcontinental variety, not very different from what I spoke. 'No,' I told her in English.

'I see,' she said, though it was clear that she didn't believe me. I guess I was classified as an enemy in her mind. Most probably she was at that point wondering if she should get out the largest kitchen knife they had, preferably one with a curved tip, and stab me to death, just to play it safe.

'We ought to call up one of your husband's friends,' I repeated. I had no idea how much she was aware of Junaid's activities.

'I don't think so. I don't want to do that anyway. How did this really happen?'

I was a bit shocked by how fluent her English was. It was Punjabi accented, but fluent nevertheless. So Junaid's missus was educated and probably very clever and it made sense that she didn't buy my explanation that Junaid had hurt himself after a verbal and very intellectual argument with me. 'We had a fight,' I told her gently. 'I was lucky.' Most women don't take kindly to being told that the husband had been worsted in a fight, especially if the person telling the wife happened to own the fist that was responsible. Junaid's wife was no different. She looked at me with shock and fear.

'If you like, I'll go to my room. If you were to sprinkle some water on his face, he'll come to.'

I started to leave. 'No, don't leave. Please. He'll blame me anyway.'

'Is that always the case?'

My question was answered by an impatient shrug. 'Where are you from?' I asked.

'Lahore.'

Lahore, the most cultured city in the Punjab, the capital of undivided Punjab before Partition. I was half Punjabi – from my mother's side. Maybe Junaid's wife was a distant cousin. Maybe Junaid himself was a cousin. I shuddered. I still hadn't come to terms with the fact that I was talking to Junaid's wife. I had assumed that Junaid's wife would either be someone from a background very similar to Junaid – born and bred in the UK, from a very orthodox family and with a very conservative outlook towards life, with a Cockney accent to boot, all wrapped snugly in a burkha, or someone imported from Pakistan, with zero knowledge of English and a total inability to converse with a stranger. I had thought that it was much more likely to be the latter. Now that I was faced with a cultured Lahori woman who was fluent in English, I felt discomfited.

'Tell me,' I asked her savagely. 'When you married Junaid, did you know what you were getting into? Did your parents know where they were sending you off to? Do they now know what sort of life you lead?'

The eyes that peered out of the burkha hardened. They were angry eyes. Was the anger directed towards me? But then they suddenly turned sad.

'I'm really sorry,' I said.

Junaid was showing signs of life. 'What's your name?' I asked the wife.

'Nilofer.'

'I'm Ritwik. Ritwik Kumar. Listen, you'd better get some water and sprinkle it on your husband. He won't remember much. Tell him you heard sounds of someone rushing into the house and came to look and found him inside. Don't tell him you've spoken with me.' The last bit was needless I was sure. Nilofer was as likely to tell Junaid that she had been chatting with me as admit that she had been committing adultery in her thoughts.

'When he went to the garden he asked me to stay inside the bedroom, unless he told me I could leave.'

'Maybe you came to the kitchen to cook?'

She shook her head. 'He was to tell me when I could go to the kitchen this morning.'

I shook my head impatiently. Junaid's eyes were starting to flicker. 'Just tell him you heard a loud thud and came to look. He won't mind this time. He might ask you to fetch his mobile so that he can call someone. Now go ahead and sprinkle some water on him.'

I rushed away. I went to my room and sat down on the bed. I was tempted to lock myself in. It took me a few minutes to compose myself, after which I went to the living room, sat down on the sofa and waited for Ayub to arrive.

# 7

IT WAS MUNIR RATHER THAN Ayub who arrived first. Did Junaid call Munir first? I don't know. I expected Munir to be full of concern for Junaid as he rushed to the kitchen looking for him. Instead, he was angry with Junaid. I could hear him berating Junaid for having got into a fight with me. After giving Junaid an earful, he came over to me and asked, 'Did he hurt you?'

'I think one of my ribs is broken.'

'We have a doctor. I'll ask him to come and take a look at that.' I was not surprised. Among the legions of supporters they had all over the world, the Taliban and al Qaeda surely had at least one British doctor at their beck and call.

'That would be good,' I said, though I was sure that without access to a hospital or some decent medical equipment, a GP with a briefcase was unlikely to be able to do much for me, except maybe administer some painkillers.

Munir went back to the kitchen while I continued to sit on the sofa. I wondered what sort of damage Junaid had sustained. There was bound to be a big bump on his forehead. Could there be any brain damage, I wondered. I was in no hurry to meet him.

Ayub arrived thirty minutes later. Unlike Munir, he spent a long time talking to Junaid who was still in the kitchen. He then came over to the living room and asked me angrily, 'Why did you provoke Junaid?'

'I could have killed him, but I didn't.'

'If you'd killed him, you could've got a piece of lead in your forehead. You might still get it.' After a pregnant pause, he continued, 'Ritwik, don't push us too much. We are already regretting having brought you to our side. You have very little information that is of any value. Tell me one good reason why we shouldn't dump you now.'

'If you do and General West gets hold of me, the police will be here in no time.'

'Oh no! I didn't mean asking you to walk away from here. Not after we have put in so much effort in bringing you here blindfolded. No, I mean, dumping you in the garden in a deep ditch. Or taking you out in a body bag in the car and tossing you into the Thames!'

Christ! Was Ayub angry!

'Look, Junaid tried to kill me. I defended myself. What did you expect me to do if someone attacks to kill?'

'You shouldn't have provoked him,' Ayub repeated like a pesky schoolboy.

'I didn't.'

'Like hell you didn't. I've known Junaid far too long! He wouldn't have hit you unless you said something to provoke him.'

'Tell me, Ayub, do you approve of the way Junaid treats his wife?'

'That's none of my business. Or your business for that matter.'

'If the police were to get an inkling of how Junaid treats his…wife,' I almost said 'Nilofer' before I remembered that I wasn't supposed to know her name, 'they will arrest him and put him in jail.'

'And do you propose to call the police? Go on. Call them up and tell them – I am Ritwik Kumar, an Indian spy, on secondment to the Foreign Office, I defected to the Taliban… or maybe you should say the al Qaeda – it is much better known, isn't it? I defected to the al Qaeda a few days ago. Now I have discovered that one of the organisation's operatives in London treats his wife pretty badly. Beats her up once in a while. Why don't you come over and arrest him? Yeah, tell them that and they might give Junaid a warning and a suspended sentence. And maybe make him do some community service in the process. That'll make him a better human being and you would have done your bit for women's rights. Go on, mate, do it! Go on!'

Ayub was silent for a bit. 'For Chrissakes, let's get our priorities right. Here you have Junaid, a born killer, a man who went to Afghanistan to serve the Cause and because he was so good they sent him back to London, as there aren't enough good people here. And you provoke Junaid by questioning his behaviour in his own home and wonder what will happen if the police were to find out how he treats his wife!'

I was silent. Ayub paced up and down the living room.

'For God's sake, man, Junaid could have killed you with a single blow. The only reason you are alive today is because Junaid was ordered to look after you and keep you alive, rather than merely prevent you from escaping.' Ayub continued to walk up and down the living room.

'I think one of my ribs is broken. I need to see a doctor. Munir said it could be arranged.' I wasn't too sure if Ayub would want me to see a doctor, but I wanted to change the subject.

'Like hell you need to see a doctor.' An amused expression came to Ayub's face. 'The best cure for a broken rib is plenty of rest. Surely you know that?'

Seeing me upset, he said, 'Let me see what can be done.'

I could hear footsteps. Munir came into the room supporting Junaid who had an egg-like lump on his forehead and a murderous look in his eyes.

'I have requested Junaid-bhai to forgive you. We are all working for the same cause and we can ill-afford to fight with each other. We will *not* fight each other. Is that understood?'

I nodded, bent my head in a gesture of submission and looked up slyly. Junaid now looked like one who thinks it beneath him to fight someone like me, when he had dedicated himself to a worthier cause.

'Listen,' I told Ayub, 'if only you guys would send me to Afghanistan, I could do something for you people there. And what about Karim? Have you decided to lose such a good guy? I just can't believe that—'

'A final decision is yet to be taken on all these things. I am not the decision maker, Ritwik. So be patient, will you? And be good, okay?'

I decided to be both – patient and good. Especially since I had the luxury of choice in the matter.

# 8

THAT NIGHT AS I SLEPT IN THAT gloomy bedroom with the large window fitted with a burglar alarm, I dreamt that I was lying under an apple tree on a bed of snow and someone was shaking the branches with a loud knocking sound.

Knock, knock! Rap! Rap! 'Wake up, Ritwik,' the angel's rasping voice pleaded with me.

It's only a dream, I told myself as I decided to sleep on. I even kept my eyes shut tight so that the dream would continue.

Knock, knock. 'Please wake up.'

I finally woke up, the knocking on the window was so insistent, though not too loud. Walking to the window I saw there was a full moon outside. Nilofer was standing in the snow-covered garden, just outside my window. In any event, the woman wearing a burkha looked like Nilofer.

As I gathered my wits, I saw her signal to me that I should open the window. I waved her away. There's a burglar alarm that'll go off if the window is opened, I gestured to her. The poor thing probably didn't have a clue what a burglar alarm was and she continued to insist. I tried once more to tell her that I couldn't. Finally I got so fed up that I decided to open it quickly, tell her to leave and deal with Junaid when he storms into my bedroom. I would tell him that I had opened the window to get some fresh air and try to look innocent. It must have been minus two degrees outside, with ankle-high snow on the ground and Junaid, fresh from the wars, a bruise on his forehead, would doubtless have agreed with me that it was perfect weather to open the window and get some fresh air.

I switched on the lights and undid the catch on the window. I slowly opened a few notches and waited with bated breath for the alarm to go off. It didn't. Instead I heard Nilofer calmly say, 'I just wanted to make sure that you aren't hurt. Are you in pain?'

'The alarm will go off any moment.'

'What?'

'This window is wired with a burglar alarm. The alarm will go off any moment. You must go back or you'll get into trouble.' The alarm didn't go off.

'Don't worry, I've switched off the alarm.'

'What?'

'I've switched off the alarm. Don't worry.'

She was quite something, this Nilofer!

'I've got you some painkillers. Here.' She held out a couple of white tablets on her palm. 'They'll put you to sleep. You won't feel the pain.'

'Where did you get them from?'

'Munir-bhai got some for my husband. I heard Ayub-bhai tell Munir-bhai to not give you any. Munir-bhai wanted to fetch a doctor for you as well. Ayub-bhai told him not to. So I thought you should....'

I could have hugged her as she struggled to explain why she had brought me the painkillers. And all along, I was thinking that Ayub was a gentleman. I took the two tablets and asked, 'Why don't you come inside? Will he wake up?'

'No. He took three of these tablets. He won't wake up anytime soon.' After a few seconds' thought, she gingerly said, 'No, I don't think I'll come inside.'

'It's cold outside. You can't stand there for long.'

'I'll go now. You take those tablets. I couldn't get you more; my husband would have noticed.'

'But we've got to talk, you and I. We are both in trouble. Please come in.'

Nilofer hesitated. I put the tablets into my mouth and held out my hand. She took it tentatively and slowly hitched up the ends of her burkha. Her hands were so cold. The base of the window was just above my knees, but the garden was a foot below the level of the floor. I tightened my grip on Nilofer's hand, hoisted her into the room and shut the window behind her.

'How did you know about the burglar alarm?' I asked.

'I was with my husband when Ayub-bhai taught him how to set it and to turn it on and off.'

'There might be a camera somewhere inside the room.'

'Not inside this room. It's in the living room actually and it focuses on that door.' Nilofer pointed a burkha-covered arm towards the door. 'It records everything and there's someone somewhere who monitors it twenty-four hours a day. They'll know if you walk out of that door.'

This was a huge unexpected bonus from a least expected quarter. 'We are safe inside here, aren't we?'

'Yes, we are, but I need to go back soon.'

I felt surreal, standing there in the middle of the night, talking to Nilofer in English, the curtain-less window behind us, as the full moon shone outside, making the snow sparkle like a fairy ground.

'Listen, I know you are unhappy. You can't possibly be happy. Why don't you leave him?'

'What sort of question is that?'

'You are educated. Your husband ill-treats you. You ought to run away.'

At that Nilofer flared up. 'Where can I go to? I can't go back to my parents. I can't live on my own,'

'Why not?'

'I went to Lahore University. I have a degree in sociology. How useful can that be?'

'In the UK, you could still get a job. Some job. Work for a supermarket. Something. You just need to leave!'

'But what will my parents think?' A million questions were answered by that single question. The desperate need for South Asians to seek parental approval in everything they do is unfathomable for a thinking human being, unless one is South Asian of course.

'Why did you marry a guy like Junaid in the first place?' I demanded.

'He is distantly related to me. They said he is a businessman. He used to run a restaurant earlier.'

'What does he do these days?'

'Nothing much except what Ayub-bhai asks him to do.'

'Where does he get his money from?'

'I don't know. We have enough money. I don't know where it comes from.'

'Where's this house located?'

'Why? Don't you know that?'

'No I don't. What's the closest tube station?'

'Mile End.'

I whistled. They had driven me around a bit and then driven me back to where that car started from.

'How close are we to the tube station?'

'Not far. It's a ten-minute walk I'd say.'

'Do you go out much?'

There was silence. 'There was a time when I used to, but now I don't.'

'Why is that?'

'I don't know. My husband doesn't like me going out very often.'

We were both silent for some time. I was lost for words. I wasn't sure if Nilofer knew what her husband was involved in.

'Didn't you want any water? For the tablets I mean?' Nilofer asked.

'I was so pleasantly surprised at seeing you that I swallowed them without water.' And Nilofer laughed shyly at that.

We laughed.

'Have you always worn the burkha?'

'No. Only after my husband started doing namaaz five times a day.'

'You mean, you didn't wear it when you lived in Pakistan?'

Nilofer smiled and shook her head in reply.

Sympathy for Nilofer clashed with my need to focus on survival. I wasn't in Ayub's or Junaid's good books. There was precious little I could do to help Nilofer and if I tried anything and got caught, I would be lucky to say a prayer before I was killed.

'You don't have any children, do you?'

'No. And I am to blame for that.'

I let that pass. 'Does Junaid have any family here in London?'

'Yes, he does. Lots of them. They are all in and around Southall. We used to live with them when my husband ran that restaurant. We moved here after my husband sold that business.'

I whistled. 'From West London to the East End. Why didn't your husband want to stay close to his family? Why move so far away?'

Nilofer sighed instead of answering.

'Don't they visit you often? Or do you visit them?'

'No, not really. My husband is no longer on such good terms with them. He… well, after he turned religious a few years ago, he went to Pakistan. He was there for a year and I was in Southall with his relatives. I didn't dare tell my parents that my husband wasn't with me. They would have been shocked if they'd come to know he was in Pakistan doing god knows what. When he returned, he was totally transformed. He doesn't like people who are not very religious around him these days. He…'

'Did you start wearing the burkha after that?'

'Yes.'

'Junaid insisted you do?'

Nilofer hesitated and said, 'I didn't mind.'

Like hell she didn't. 'Why don't you take off that burkha?' I said on an impulse.

'What? Of course no! No.'

'Why not? You are a human being. I am a human being, I can't really talk to you if you are wrapped up in that.'

She stared at me in silence. I stared back. 'Please take it off.'

She slowly took off the top of her burkha that covered her head like an evil envelope and held it in her hand. I was stunned. I was not sure what I had expected Nilofer to look like, but the woman who stood in front of me was beautiful. Not in a conventional sense, though. Her face wasn't as plump as I had imagined her to be, and her cheekbones stood out which made me suspect that underneath the rest of the burkha, she was very thin. She looked like a little girl. A little girl lost. She looked so very lost.

We stared at each other for a while. Then with a small cry, Nilofer quickly put the burkha back on and started to leave. I was too startled to help her. She quickly opened the window and jumped out of it. 'Sleep well,' she told me and soon she was gone, like an elf over the snow.

# 9

'I'VE BROUGHT SOMEONE TO meet you,' Ayub told me with a grin when he came to see me the next day. He was, as usual, well-dressed in a cashmere sweater and an expensive overcoat that was in sharp contrast to my cheap but comfortable Primark sweater that could be described as either blue or green, depending on the beholder.

I looked around politely and found no one other than Junaid who had his usual blank expression on his face, despite the small bulge above his eye.

'And where have you hidden this person?' I asked as I looked under the sofa.

'Guess?'

Ayub was looking happy, as though he was in the mood for some fun.

'It must be a travel agent then,' I said. 'Someone who can get me to Afghanistan.'

'You're close. Keep guessing.' At this even Junaid gave me an encouraging smile.

'I give up!' I threw up my hands.

Ayub gave me a nod, then another and started to open his briefcase. His mannerisms were so much that of a public school boy educated at any of the best schools in the world. I wanted to grab him by his shoulders and tell him, 'Ayub Afridi, you idiot, wake up. You don't belong here.'

'Are you sure you don't want to take another shot. It's not a thing. It's an individual. Someone you'll get very close to in the next couple of weeks.'

'A photograph of an individual?'

'You're almost there.'

Before I could say any further, Ayub took a green passport out of his suitcase and threw it on my lap.

'A Pakistani passport.'

'It belongs to one Sajid Khan.' I opened the pages and looked at Sajid Khan's mugshot. A bearded man, Sajid seemed to be roughly my age. 'Born on 30 March 1961.' I looked up at Ayub.

'That's just a year younger than you. This is the best we could do.'

Realisation slowly dawned on me. 'You want me to travel with this passport? You've got to be nuts. I'll never get away with it.'

'You'll have to.'

'What if I refuse to travel with this?'

'Trust me, if you do that, you'll be out on the streets in no time at all. Our boys haven't been very impressed with you. One would expect a defector of your calibre to have had some more useful stuff to tell us. Once you are out on the streets, you'll remain there till you get caught. Which won't be very long, considering that there's an-all out alert for you. You'll go to jail for a very long time.'

'Hey, relax! I just wanted to know what my options are.'

Ayub seemed to be amused by my question, 'You don't have many. In fact, you have exactly two options. One – you can do what we ask you to do. Else, you can get your arse out of here and—'

'Listen, if I travel out of here on a Pakistani passport, someone's going to be interested in me. Can't you get me an Indian passport?'

Ayub laughed and Junaid laughed with him. 'You want us to get you an Indian passport?'

'Well, look at this photograph,' I said as I tapped Sajid's snap with my forefinger. 'It'll take me a month to grow so much hair on my jaw. A month if I'm lucky. Also, I don't have so much grey hair.'

'Come on. Don't be silly. We'll get you a wig. We have done that many times before. As for greying your hair, make sure you don't stand under a shower after our makeup artists do some work on you.'

'But Indian passports are not so difficult to get hold of,' I protested. 'And they attract so much less attention. Compared to a Pakistani passport, I mean.'

'And where do you think you are flying off to, with an Indian passport?'

'Afghanistan?'

'That's your ultimate destination. But no, you don't fly to Afghanistan from Heathrow.' Ayub was silent for a moment and he then continued. 'You fly to Pakistan from here. To Islamabad. And from Islamabad you go to Pindi where we have friends. You stay in a safe-house like this and someone will take you to Afghanistan.' Visions of travelling from Rawalpindi to Afghanistan in a colourful truck with a cheerful, gold-toothed, loud-mouthed truck driver for company came to my mind.

'Why can't I travel to Pakistan on an Indian passport?' I asked and immediately felt very stupid. I knew the answer to that one. I would need a Pakistani visa to begin with, something that could take a fair amount of time. More importantly, on landing in Pakistan, I could expect the sort of scrutiny that in the UK would normally be reserved for someone from Saudi Arabia with bin Laden for a surname.

'Fine! How about a Sri Lankan passport? Or a Nepali one?'

'And why would a Sri Lankan want to travel to Islamabad? Or a Nepali for that matter? They'll unravel your story in a matter of minutes.'

I had to concede that they were right. If I travelled to Pakistan as Sajid Khan, a Pakistani returning home after a visit to the UK, I was going to attract a lot less attention than I would otherwise.

'The best thing is that this is a genuine passport with a British visa valid for another four months. Sajid has come to the UK to visit his family and will not need his passport for another couple of months. Once you reach Pakistan, someone else will use it to travel to the UK so that Sajid can fly back home.' Ayub said sounding supremely confident.

'I've got an idea,' I told Ayub. 'Something that will largely increase my chances of getting away without being caught.'

'Tell me, Ritwik, I'm all for a good idea. Anything that will get you to Afghanistan in one piece, without having to enjoy Her Majesty's hospitality or that of the Pakistani government is fine with me. You may even get to work on Karim. Someone high-up has almost decided that he shouldn't be just killed. You might prove your worth after all.'

'That's fantastic news. If I get to spend ten minutes with Karim, I can explain to him how I misled him. He is a good guy. You guys shouldn't waste him, just like that.'

'Hold on. Nothing's been decided yet. These things may take some more time. Now what's this brilliant idea that you've got?'

'Yes, you see, if I were to travel with my wife, the chances of raising suspicions would be a lot less, right?'

'You are a dirty son-of-a-bitch. But as it happens, only Sajid Khan has made the journey from home. His wife is waiting for him to get back to Pakistan.'

'Surely, his wife has a passport, nice and genuine.'

'Ah I see. You are not happy with the sacrifice Sajid-bhai is making for you. You want to put his wife at risk as well. You want her to travel to London and travel back with you? Is that what you had in mind?'

Ayub was irritated, and Junaid looked angry.

'No, that's not what I had in mind. I thought Mrs Khan could mail her passport to you. And someone else could use it to travel back with me.'

'You have someone else in mind? You know someone here in London who will pretend to be your wife and travel to Pakistan with you?' Ayub looked astonished. Junaid looked even more bugged.

'Well, Junaid-bhai has already contributed so much to the cause and so I don't have the heart to suggest that his wife should also pitch in and do her li'l bit—'

Before Junaid could get to me, Ayub had whipped his Glock 17 semiautomatic out of his jacket and hit me on the back of my head. I really wasn't expecting it from Ayub. I crumbled forward.

Junaid towered over me and looked like he would like to tear me up into bits and pieces.

'Don't kill him, but you may hit him once. Just once. In his stomach.'

Junaid looked at Ayub as if he couldn't believe his ears. He looked like an eager fifteen-year old.

'Ritwik, if you try to move, I'll kill you,' Ayub warned me as I lay with my head thrown back on the sofa, grimacing with pain, my right hand gently massaging the back of my head.

Junaid came towards me, a smile on his lips, a martyr about to receive his just reward from the heavens above. I sat slumped forward, my head and body too stunned to move or resist. I had drawn up my legs in a foetal position. As Junaid was close enough, my right leg shot forward and caught Junaid's knee cap, his left one, if I remember right. The sound made by my shoe as it made acquaintance with Junaid's knee was drowned by a cry of agony as Junaid crumbled to the floor.

My glory didn't last for long. Ayub poked me on the left side, not far from my bruised rib. The butt of the Glock 17 is made of steel and Ayub didn't try too hard to reduce the impact. Rather, I think he put the entire weight of his body behind the blow and though he was not as tough as Junaid, I felt as if a cannonball had hit me in my side. This time I was fully immobilised as I slumped forward. My mouth twisted in agony. In that state, I wouldn't have been able to kick Junaid or anyone else even if they had been tranquillised and planted in front of me.

Junaid slowly got back to his feet, holding to the sofa for support.

'Don't you dare touch him now,' Ayub told Junaid. 'I've had to do your job for you!' He then turned to me and said, 'When you are able to, go to your room. We'll talk again tomorrow. You'll be travelling to Pakistan in a few days from now. Make sure you recover by then.' With that and a laugh, Ayub left, taking Sajid's passport with him.

Junaid started at me, more with wonder than anything else. How did you muster the courage to kick me when Ayub-bhai had ordered you to stay still, he seemed to ask me.

# 10

THE DOCTOR WHO CAME TO look at me was a young man, in his early thirties, very obviously a convert to Ayub's and Junaid's cause. He had a beard as long as Junaid's, though his outgrowth was nowhere as thick or luxuriant. His hairline was receding and he had plastered long strands of his hair all over his scalp in an effort to cover the bald patches, quite a contrast to Junaid whose head was covered with a thick carpet of very short hair. Again, unlike Junaid who seemed to be very comfortable with his beard, the doctor kept playing with his all the time, twirling the ends with itchy fingers and twisting them into thin, long strands. He evidently hadn't been told who I was or how I had been hurt and he kept looking at me with a puzzled expression, trying to figure out if I was one of the good guys who had been injured while fighting the infidels or an infidel being held prisoner. Junaid stood beside me while the doctor examined me. After the doctor had prodded me in my ribs a few times, made me moan in pain, felt the bump on the back of my head and made me moan yet again, I decided to do my best to give the impression that Ayub and I were bosom buddies.

'When's Ayub's expected?' I asked Junaid in the friendliest manner possible.

Junaid didn't expect such a question from me. He was silent for a bit and then replied, 'No idea.'

'That boy, he works too hard. He ought to take it easy,' I continued.

'Hmmm.' Junaid's lips had hardly moved.

'Did Ayub ever tell you he got hurt in a very similar fashion when he used to be in Kabul?'

'I don't know.' Junaid was visibly bugged with me and I could imagine the wheels in his brain trying to churn out an adequate response to my tactics. The doctor on the other hand, was not in the know, and was very eager for as much information as possible.

'Afghanistan is no longer a safe place for our people,' he said wistfully.

'You won't believe how Ayub got hurt,' I told the two men.

'Maybe you should keep quiet,' Junaid suggested, the menace in the voice barely hidden. He was happy he had managed to articulate a response. 'Yes, you shouldn't speak so much. It's not good for you,' he added more gently, his eyes lit up with pride at his creativity.

I looked at the good doctor for sympathy and support. Having completed his examination, the worthy young man was all set to give me an injection, something anti-inflammatory, I presumed. Junaid's stern expression now extended to the doctor, and he hastily piped in, 'Yes, it's not a good idea to talk so much. You ought to take it easy. Doesn't it hurt when you speak?'

'Yes, it does,' I conceded. Heck, it hurt not only when I spoke, but even when I took a deep breath. I was pretty sure that I had cracked a rib. Maybe two. These were in addition to the bruises Junaid had inflicted on my ribs two days ago in the garden.

The doctor's accent was very much Brummie. I wondered when he had turned an al Qaeda activist. Was he recruited in Birmingham or was it after he moved to London that he joined the cause? Maybe he hadn't moved to London at all. Maybe he had travelled all the way from Birmingham just to see me, on Ayub's orders.

'How long will it be before he is able to travel?' Junaid asked the doctor who was many shades darker than Junaid. Is he of Bengali origin, I wondered. Not that it made any difference to me or to anyone else. Bengali or Punjabi, Indian or Sri Lankan, Caucasian or African, once an individual fell into the al Qaeda's ideological clutches, he was as pliable a tool as ever existed in the world of power politics. The Nazis in Germany and the Communists in the Soviet Union had many such pawns. They also had many very clever operators, men like Ayub and yet they had lost. I had personally worked with many intelligent Soviet agents. None of them had been able to prevent the Soviet Union from hurrying into its grave. Would Islamic fundamentalism decline and die as had happened with the Nazis and the Commies? I could only wish that it would, though for the moment, I was on the side of the al Qaeda. I was glad that my parents, god rest their souls in peace, were not alive to see me thus.

'He should rest for ideally a month. But he should be able to travel in two weeks' time.'

'Can you tell me how many ribs have been broken?' I asked the doctor.

'Oh dear. It's so difficult to say that without an x-ray and you know we can't get an x-ray. It's possible a rib is broken and another two are bruised. Maybe two ribs are broken, maybe two ribs are bruised, maybe.'

'Basically, you don't know!' I gasped.

'That's right,' the doctor agreed cheerfully, and stood up.

I got three small white packets full of medicines, each of them labelled with dosage instructions. The doctor left them on the coffee table that was sandwiched between two sofas that faced each other. I was hoping that Junaid would see the doctor out. Ayub was not around. I could hear Nilofer in the kitchen. What was I planning to do? Rush into the kitchen and have a quick word with Nilofer when Junaid's back was turned? And what would I tell her? That I found her very pretty and wanted to talk to her at length. That I wanted to spend more time with her? Take her out for a walk? Hug her? For god's sake man, I told myself. I was in my very late forties and Nilofer was unlikely to be a day over thirty.

Junaid did get up and see the doctor out. I restrained myself from doing anything stupid. If Nilofer didn't really like what her husband did, then she was unlikely to find a man who had defected to Junaid's side attractive. Granted I was not personally a fundamentalist, but I had jumped to their side and was all set to travel to Afghanistan to work for them.

Junaid came back and sat down on the sofa next to me. He fished out his mobile phone and dialled a number. Why don't you play with your beard just like that doctor did? I wanted to ask him, but desisted.

'The doctor says he must rest for a month, but he can travel in two weeks' time.'

Junaid's forehead furrowed as he listened intently to what the other person was saying. He then said 'Okay' and ended the call.

'Ayub-bhai says Sajid Khan will travel from London Heathrow to Islamabad in ten days' time. He's asked me to book the tickets.'

I tried to look happy. 'That sounds just fine. I should be able to get my one month's rest once I am in Pakistan, I guess.'

'I don't know. I guess.' Junaid, I was sure, would never be told anything more than he needed to know. He would always be a foot soldier and would be happy being a foot soldier.

'Any news from Munir? Where has he disappeared to?' I hadn't seen Munir since the day I had my tussle with Junaid in the garden.

'Munir-bhai is busy with his work and his work for the cause.'

'What does Munir do, I mean, when he is not working for the cause?'

'You aren't to know that.'

'Why is that?' I asked exasperated. 'I am one of you now, am I not? How can I work with you all if I don't know anything about any of you?'

'That's what I've been told.' Junaid sounded a trifle sad, and it was all too obvious that he had no clue why he had been instructed to not tell me anything.

'Can you ask Ayub if I can go for a walk?'

'But you shouldn't walk around,' he protested, looking a bit concerned.

'Fine, I'll rest. But I'd like to know if I am allowed to go for a walk. It's the principle of the thing. If I weren't hurt, could I have gone for a walk?'

'I don't know.'

'You don't know?'

'No,' Junaid conceded. 'You can't go for a walk. Ayub-bhai said that even before you broke your ribs. You can't leave this house.'

'Why is that?'

'Because Ayub-bhai says so.'

I gave up. At that very moment, the door bell rang. It was obviously an unexpected caller. Junaid looked around curiously. Saying 'Someone's at the door,' he got up and went to open the door. The moment he stepped out of the room, Nilofer rushed in from the kitchen with some things in each of her hands. With a very Bollywoodish 'sssssshhh' that couldn't have been heard beyond five feet, she shoved the objects in her hands inside my sweater, except for a small key she held on to as she ran away. Before I could say anything or react in any other way, she was gone, the soft patter of her bare feet barely making a sound. Clever girl, I thought. She had even taken off her shoes! And that key must be for the small door that led from the garden in the rear to the courtyard in the front of the house.

Junaid came back a few minutes later, looking thoroughly annoyed and sat down on the sofa opposite me.

'There was no one at the door.'

I raised an eyebrow at him.

'Neighbourhood kids having fun?'

'No, I don't think so. There's a gate that's padlocked. They couldn't have—'

'Maybe it was a salesman who rang the bell and then changed his mind?'

'No, no one can open the outer gate. The bell is at the door.'

I figured that the courtyard in front of the house was wide enough to prevent the bell from being rung without entering the courtyard.

'Maybe a bird sat on the bell?'

'No, it's just a switch, you see. A bird could not have sat on it.'

'Maybe you imagined it?'

'Imagined it?' Junaid looked shocked.

'Well, did you hear the bell?'

'I did, didn't you?'

'Not really. You did say "someone's at the door" when you got up and went, but I wasn't paying much attention and so I thought I had just missed the bell.'

'You mean…' Junaid gulped. Most probably he was planning to inform Ayub about the incident. I could see him turn it over in his head. On the one hand he was a loyal foot soldier. On the other hand, he knew very well that Ayub would not have much patience with someone who imagined bells ringing.

'Are you sure you didn't hear the bell ring?' Junaid asked me.

'No,' I said slowly. 'I don't think so. But then I wasn't paying much attention. Maybe it did ring.'

I picked up the three small white packets of medicines and put them into the pockets of my sweater. 'I think I'll go and get some rest. I pray to god I feel better in ten days' time. Couldn't Ayub have asked you to book the tickets after a month? After all, isn't that what the doctor said?'

'Ritwik-bhai, you asked for trouble and you got it,' Junaid smirked, but I could see that his self-confidence was now at an all-time low.

I am a man who is all for conceding defeat when the situation so warrants. I gave Junaid a defeated grin and slowly got up with my hands inside the side pockets of my sweater, gripping my hips, so that whatever Nilofer had put inside my sweater wouldn't fall out. I carefully walked to my room and shut the door behind me. I sat on the bed and took out the two solid objects. One was a mobile phone and the other its charger, with the wires all wound up around the plug.

The mobile was fully charged. I started to go through the list of contacts and found lots of South Asian Muslim names. In fact, they were all South Asian Muslim names. I looked for Ayub and didn't find his name. Junaid was also conspicuous by his absence. I then looked for 'Munir' and found it. Munir was a contact. Nilofer Ali too was listed as a contact. I hesitated. Should I dial Nilofer's number? I decided not to. Nilofer might be with Junaid. No, Nilofer would call me when she was on her own.

I started to scroll through the names from A to Z and found an Afridi. It had to be Ayub, I was sure. Most of the contacts, like Munir, were listed by the first name and the rest, like Ayub, by just the surname. Only Nilofer had her full name listed. Nilofer Ali showed ownership. I was sure that Ali was not her maiden name. I changed the ringer option to vibrate and put the mobile back into my pocket. The charger went into the other pocket. I got into bed fully dressed and waited for my mobile phone to vibrate.

An hour later, the cellphone vibrated. I eagerly took the mobile out of my pocket. A London landline number starting with 0208 showed on the screen.

'Hello?'

'It's me, Nilofer,' said the sweetest voice in the world.

# 11

'THAT WAS A HELL OF A RISK you took,' I told Nilofer.

'I don't care. These days I don't really care.'

'You don't even know what I'm up to.'

'I know that you are my husband's prisoner. Well, not exactly, but you can't leave the house if you want to....'

'What if Junaid had found out that it was you who rang the bell?'

'How could he? He doesn't have more than a pair of eyes.'

'Where did you get hold of an extra mobile phone?'

'When my husband upgraded his phone last year, he switched his old one to pay-as-you-go, in case he needed a spare one.'

'So I'm using Junaid's old phone, am I?

Nilofer giggled in response.

'Won't he miss it?'

'No, he won't. He doesn't use it.'

'You are calling me from your landline. Don't you have a mobile phone? You ought to lock yourself inside a toilet and call me from your cellphone.'

'I don't have a cellphone.'

'Did you ever have one?'

'Yes, I used to. When we lived in Southall.'

The mobile number listed under Nilofer was probably her old number. Why don't you have one now? I wanted to ask, but I didn't. Instead I said, 'So I'm on pay-as-you-go, am I? How much credit do I have?'

'Not much. Around five pounds I think. You don't need any. I'll call you when I can.'

'Where's Junaid right now?'

'He's listening to the radio in his room.'

'And where are you?'

'In the kitchen.'

'What if Junaid comes to the kitchen and finds you on the phone?'

'I could be speaking to my parents. I call them once in a while.'

'Do you call them often?'

'It's usually once a week. Usually on a Friday when my Abba is at home. But there is no set rule. I call them whenever I feel like. So, if my husband sees me on the phone, I can say I am calling home.'

'It's good that Junaid lets you call home as often as you like. Do you use a calling plan?'

'Yes.' She mentioned one of those cheap call operators who allow users with an account to dial a free phone number and talk to anyone in India or Pakistan at very low rates.

'What if Junaid looks at your telephone bill next month and sees so many phone calls to his old mobile number?'

'He won't notice. He makes so many calls from our home number to so many people. I think he gets a lot of money from Ayub-bhai to pay for all this. So, he never checks.'

'What if he does?'

'Don't worry. You are worrying too much.' I had to agree, I was.

'There are certain things my husband does and certain things he doesn't, certain things that upset him and certain things which don't. Don't worry, he won't find out and I know my husband very well.'

I hoped to hell she was right. 'Well, please don't take too many risks.'

'You are worrying too much. I'll be fine.' Now Nilofer sounded exasperated.

Thanks to the mobile phone, I became pretty cheerful. The ten-day wait before I could travel to Pakistan went by rather fast. Nilofer called me at least once a day, sometimes twice. We became friends. I got to know of her parents too. Her abba – a hardworking businessman who did wholesale trading in pistachios and almonds, was very liberal, bought bootlegged whiskey from local Christians and counted Hindus, Parsees, Mohajirs, Shias and Ahmediyas among his friends;

her mother, an equally hardworking housewife who had at one time taught in a school; her elder brother, a major in the Pakistani army; her elder sister happily married to a bureaucrat in Islamabad with three kids; her two younger sisters, one married to a school teacher, another to a man who worked for their father's business; and her youngest sibling, a lad of twenty, still at university.

The weather was still cold but it had stopped snowing. The snow that lay on the ground started to melt a bit in the daytime, but froze at night, when the temperature dipped below zero. The garden was still blanketed in white, though in a few places the brown earth could be seen.

Nilofer never asked me what I was up to with Ayub, Junaid and company, which surprised me. However, she was infinitely curious in knowing why I was still single.

'I never got around to it,' I told her.

'You are still looking for the right one, hunh?'

'Not any more. At one point I was, but not anymore.'

'But you should have someone.'

'It's not easy.'

'I'm sure there was someone.'

'No, not really. Well, actually there was.'

'See, I knew. A man like you cannot have reached fifty without having met someone he likes.'

'Hey, I'm not fifty yet.'

'But you are almost there, aren't you?' Nilofer laughed, a teasing, merry, innocent laugh.

'Tell me about her,' Nilofer chirped.

'The girl I almost married? She was also a diplomat like

me. An Indian diplomat. We dated for a while, made plans to get married, but nothing came of it.'

'She must have been very clever like you. What was her name?'

'Soumya.'

'Did your parents object?'

'No, why should they? My parents come from mixed backgrounds. My father was a Maharashtrian and my mother a Punjabi. Soumya was from Hyderabad.'

'I know, you have a Hyderabad in India too, don't you?'

'Ha! Ha! I thought it was the other way round. You have a Hyderabad in Pakistan too!'

Nilofer giggled and said, 'Tell me, tell me, why didn't you marry?'

'It was my fault actually. I travelled around too much and could never make time for her. Finally Soumya found someone who could give her much more than I could. We are still friends. I call her once in a while.'

'That's so sad. Maybe one day she will come back to you.'

'I doubt it. She has a husband and a child.'

'You never know.'

I waited for Nilofer to ask me why I had to travel a lot and that too more than Soumya, when both of us were diplomats. She didn't. It was as if Nilofer knew what sort of questions I wouldn't be able to answer and avoided them. Did Nilofer believe Soumya's husband would die, as in a Bollywood movie, and that she could come back to me? I didn't ask.

We spoke mostly in Punjabi, Nilofer in her flowery Lahori version and me in my Jalandhari accent.

One day I asked her, 'You said you can't have kids, didn't you? Does it bother you a lot?'

'That's one of the reasons why Junaid turned to God. I think so anyway.'

'Did you undergo a lot of medical treatment?'

'Yes, I used to.'

'Did the doctors give up on you?'

'No, they didn't. They were pretty hopeful, but…'

'But?'

'My husband decided that if Allah wanted me to have a child, he would give me one.'

'I see.'

'He doesn't want to have anything to do with doctors or teachers or even his own relatives. That's why we moved so far away from them all.'

'Do you miss them?'

'Yes, even though some of them were mean to me and always teased me for being barren. Some company is better than no company at all.' Nilofer's voice broke into a sob.

'Take it easy. Let's talk about something pleasant.'

'You tell me something pleasant.'

'You know what I did to your husband.'

'I've seen what you've done to him. Poor chap. He doesn't deserve that. And I used to think he was so strong. Indestructible. He's still limping, you know?'

'No, I didn't mean that. I meant something else. Do you remember the day you went and rang the bell and then gave me the mobile?'

'Yes, of course.'

'Well that day, just after you gave me the phone and charger and went away, I got Junaid to think that he had imagined the bell ringing. That it didn't ring at all. He had imagined it.'

'How'd you manage that?'

'Junaid told me he didn't find anyone at the door and I offered him various explanations. School kids playing tricks, a salesman who changed his mind and ran away, etc. And then I told him that maybe, maybe, he had imagined the bell ringing.'

'Didn't you hear the bell ring?'

'Yes, I did. But I didn't tell him that I had heard it ring.'

'You offered him all those options and—'

'He said none of them was possible since the outer gate is locked. And then I said maybe he had imagined the bell ring.'

'He fell for that?'

'He asked me if I hadn't heard the bell ring. I said no. You see, when the bell rang, Junaid said "someone's at the door", and went off to answer the call. I later told Junaid that I hadn't heard the bell ring, but thought I had just missed it.'

'No wonder, he's had a bewildered look on his face for the last eight days!'

'Maybe you could do it once again. When Junaid and I are together in the living room, if you could ring the bell, Junaid will go to answer the door and I'll tell him I never heard the bell ring.'

'Good idea, but what if I get caught?'

I was immediately contrite. 'Please don't take any risks. It was just a thought. I hate him for the way he treats you.'

'He is still my husband.' Those words, those five words, they could have been spoken by any woman anywhere in the world. I gave up.

It would have been good fun if Junaid could be given some more food for thought, but I had no right to push Nilofer into danger. I spent most of my time sitting in the living room with Junaid, staring at the ceiling. I wished they had a TV. I wished Junaid had a bookshelf with a few books I could read. In desperation I had asked for a copy of the Koran, which Junaid had happily supplied. However, I couldn't bring myself to read the Koran for more than a few minutes at a stretch, before my mind started to wander. There were too many things for me to think of and worry about.

The evening before the day I was to travel to Islamabad, Nilofer called me for the last time. By now it was no longer so cold, the temperature was four or five degrees above zero and the snow in the garden had turned to slush. White was mixed with brown earth. I could only imagine how the roads and pavements would be. Slushy and muddy as the melted snow mixed with the dirt and grit.

'I wish we could both run away,' I told her for the umpteenth time.

'Don't worry, we'll see each other somewhere, sometime.'

'Do you believe in reincarnation?' I asked her.

'No, the Koran doesn't talk of reincarnation.'

'I know, but do you believe in it?'

'No, not really, no. It's not a bad concept, but I don't believe in it.'

'I do. I didn't until now, but now I do. And I believe that we will be together in another lifetime.'

'Why do you want to be with me in another lifetime?'

'Because I love you, Nilofer. You know that, don't you? I love you. I've loved you ever since I saw your face that night when you gave me those painkillers.' I kissed the speaker loudly, my heart beating wildly as I wondered how Nilofer would react. Steady man, you are dealing with a very young girl from Lahore, someone who's had a traditional upbringing, I told myself. There was no response for a few seconds. My heart pounded. Was Nilofer angry with me? I was all set to apologise when Nilofer kissed back.

# 12

'AT THIS RATE, I'LL MISS MY flight,' I told the company at large, which consisted of Junaid, Ayub, Munir, the driver and a young man who was to fly with me to Pakistan. I was blindfolded and was sitting on the floor, in the rear of the SUV in which we were to travel to Heathrow.

'Patience is the virtue of all great men,' Ayub counselled. 'I wonder what they want to tell me now,' he added.

I could smell each of the men in the car. Junaid was the closest to me, as he sat on the seat just behind my head and the smell of his old leather jacket almost overpowered his body odour, which could have knocked out a man. Munir was the next closest and he wore a cheap deodorant that was only mildly offensive. Ayub on the other hand exuded an expensive fragrance that must have originated from a shelf at

Harrods or Selfridges. The driver was the farthest from me. He was the same man who had driven me in the Peugeot from Mile End tube station to Junaid's house when I arrived. His hair was still shoulder-length and his beard was still neatly trimmed. At least the hair was shoulder-length and the beard was neatly trimmed when they had blindfolded me and made me sit on the floor of the SUV. The driver exuded a neutral smell, the smell of someone who is not really scared, not one-tenth as scared as I was, the smell of someone on the fringes of trouble, one who is excited and maybe even nervous, but definitely not frightened.

The young man who was to accompany me to Pakistan on the PIA flight smelt of fear and that was for a very good reason. He had been given a forged passport, a crude forgery, one that would stand out like a sore thumb in front of any Pakistani immigration official, even one who had downed a few large pegs of bootlegged whiskey. It was not that he didn't have a genuine passport, one that carried his name, photograph and signature. He did and he proposed to use his genuine Pakistani passport to travel from Heathrow to Islamabad. However, before the aircraft landed in Islamabad, he was to tear up his genuine passport, flush it down the toilet and on landing, present the forged passport, actually an apology for a forged passport, for examination and immigration clearance. I was to be standing in the queue behind him and hopefully, as the young man was discovered and arrested, not much attention would be paid to me or my passport, both of which could pass muster unless someone decided to examine either very closely. Ayub had promised to spring the young man from jail within a few days of his expected arrest and incarceration, and I was sure that he would do it.

'Can't you give them a call and ask them?' I asked Ayub petulantly. 'Why do you need to wait for them to call you back?' Ayub didn't reply and so I said, 'I still don't see why you can't let us take the tube to Heathrow on our own. Do you think I'm likely to change my mind and turn myself in? I'll probably get a life sentence, that is unless they extradite me to India, in which case I'll most probably face a firing squad at the Ambala cantonment.'

'Patience, my dear Ritwik,' Ayub repeated. I wished I could see his face as he spoke. Most probably they were all grinning with merriment at my discomfort.

'At least let me sit on the seat till they call you. This is bloody uncomfortable.'

There was silence and then Ayub ventured, 'Junaid, help him sit up.' At that, I felt Junaid's massive hands under my armpit as he helped me get up from my position on the floor and sit next to him. It had been five in the morning when they had blindfolded me and made me sit on the floor of the SUV. The driver had put the vehicle into gear and I could hear the door of the garage being opened. At that moment Ayub's mobile had rung. My mobile, the one Nilofer gave me, was stuck to the underside of my bed with a large strip of duct tape that I had 'accidentally' found under the sofa in the living room a day earlier. Ayub had spoken on the mobile for a few seconds before he got out of the SUV to continue the conversation. He returned to tell us that we had to stay put for a while before we could move. It was probably half past five by now.

'The traffic will pick up soon,' I told them.

Munir laughed at me and said, 'Like hell you'll have traffic at this time in the morning.'

Ayub joined in the merriment. 'You never know, you might have bumper-to-bumper traffic at six in the morning on a cold January morning.'

'We are bound to hit some traffic as we approach Heathrow. I know this chap who missed a flight from Heathrow on a Sunday morning. He thought there would be no traffic and took it easy and left his home in Wimbledon at six a.m., a full three hours before his flight was to take off. This was a BMI flight to Moscow. And he missed his flight. He was cruising till he got into the M25, but after that, man, was he stuck! He was so—'

'Ritwik, you have a vivid imagination,' Ayub interrupted. He then added, 'If you miss your flight, I'll put you on a chartered flight to Islamabad tonight. Is that a deal?'

I remained silent, hoping to convey how hurt and upset I was. I don't think anyone gave a damn. Another ten minutes later, Ayub's phone rang. As he had done earlier, he got out of the SUV to take the call. This time, he was on the phone for almost ten minutes I think. When he came back, he said, 'Ritwik, tough luck! You are not going to catch that flight. Everyone, get out. Back into the house.'

'Do you mind telling me what's going on?' I asked and took off my blindfold without waiting for Junaid or anyone else to do it for me. By that time, they were all out of the SUV. I gingerly jumped out. The garage was lit up very brightly and I blinked.

'Come inside, Ritwik, we need to talk. Munir-bhai, you too come inside.' Ayub had a grim look on his face, as if he were the bearer of unpleasant tidings.

'For god's sake, if PIA has cancelled its flight, let me fly BA. Or any other airline for that matter. I could fly Emirates or Itihad or Qatar, couldn't I?'

'Ritwik, I didn't say the flight has been cancelled. I only said that there has been a change of plan.'

'Like hell there has been a change of plans.'

Junaid and Munir had stepped inside the house. The young man, almost my companion on the flight I was now not going to take, started to follow them and I followed him. The driver stood near the SUV, looking undecided. 'You might as well leave now,' Ayub told him in English.

'Will you need me today? I am supposed to be at work by noon.'

'No, definitely not today. But we might need your help tomorrow. Most probably, these chaps will be travelling tomorrow.'

I took another step into the house. Junaid and Munir had disappeared. Behind me, I could sense the driver opening the door of the garage so that he could leave. I stretched out both my arms, in the manner of one whose limbs have been cramped for long.

'I can't wait to find out why there has been a change of plan,' I told Ayub as I stretched and stretched as if I were ever so cramped. Before Ayub could say anything, I spun on my heels and smashed a fist into his nose, causing him to fall flat on his back. I quickly bent down and started to unbutton his jacket so that I could get to his pistol. The driver had half opened the door of the garage. I expected him to either flee or close the door behind him and shout for help. He did none of that. Instead, he took two steps towards me and threw himself at my legs causing me to fall on to Ayub.

It was my almost-flight-companion who ruined the party for me. Hearing the commotion, he came running back from inside the house. Taking one look at the melee, he screamed, 'Junaid-bhai, Munir-bhai, please come quickly. He's escaping.' I heard the sounds of Junaid and Munir rushing back. By that time I had propped myself up. The driver lay at my feet, his arms entwined around my legs. I raised my right hand as high as I could and used the side of my palm to plant a hit on the base of his neck. It was a textbook example of how to kill a man with a single chop. The snapping sound left no doubt that the driver was dead. I ripped off Ayub's overcoat and rummaged through it for his Glock 17 semiautomatic. By the time I had it in my hand, Junaid had materialised in the doorway, his hand inside his jacket and a look of polite curiosity on his face.

I pointed the pistol at Ayub's head. That was a mistake. I ought to have pointed it at Junaid and shot him dead. 'If you come near me, I will kill him,' I told Junaid. The polite enquiring look on his face did not waver. I might as well have pointed a pistol at a mad elephant charging towards me. When Junaid appeared at the door, he had his hand inside his jacket, in the process of drawing his pistol. A second later, he had whipped out his Beretta M9, rushed towards me and hit me on the temple with it. I could have killed Ayub in that one split second, but I doubt if it would have stopped Junaid. In all probability, shooting Ayub dead would have earned me much more than the clout to my temple, which incidentally knocked me out.

When I came to, I was on my bed and Junaid and Munir were standing nearby.

'He's up,' Munir spoke over his shoulder and Ayub came into the room, his nose covered with a sticky plaster and a thin trickle of blood still visible on his upper lip. I wanted to smile, but I couldn't.

'Munir-bhai, your initial suspicions were right. Ritwik is a double agent,' Ayub told Munir with a smile.

Munir flinched and then asked him, 'You just found out?'

'Let me put it this way,' Ayub told Munir. 'We always knew that, but couldn't afford to find out till now.'

# 13

'WHY WOULD YOU SAY THAT?' I asked Ayub as indignantly as I could, despite the throbbing in my head.

'Because you are one. A double agent, I mean. A double agent is a double agent is a double agent. Now who said that, do you know?'

'Listen guys, if you want to put me through the wringer once again, I just don't have the energy for it. I'm almost fifty, in case you sweet folks have forgotten.'

'Why did you try to escape?' Munir asked me. 'If you are not a traitor, why did you want to flee? Why that sudden dash towards freedom?'

'Escape, flee, dash, are there any other verbs that you can think of? Have you been attending English language classes?

I know that you are an intellectual, but don't you think you are overdoing it?'

Munir's face reddened and we both said nothing further on that subject.

'So, he's a double agent, is he?' Munir asked Ayub once more. I knew that he was dying to ask Ayub how he knew, but he couldn't do that in my presence.

I decided to sit up in bed. It's not easy to have a discussion on whether I was a double agent or not while lying in bed. Rather than ask permission to sit, I decided to do it slowly so that Ayub would have ample time to warn me before he blew my brains out. Once I had adjusted my posterior to a reasonable degree of comfort, and leaned back against one of the vertical rods in the bedstead, I said, 'You men are assuming I am a double-crosser just because I tried to escape? That's a bit silly, isn't it? Maybe I've got a very good reason for trying to, ummm, how shall I say, for wanting to make a dash for freedom, as our good friend Munir tried to put it.'

'Go on, Ritwik, tell me why you were trying to run away. I'm all ears. *Audi alteram partem* – listen to both sides of the case, as the Romans taught us.' Ayub was once again the well-trained public schoolboy, all set to follow established democratic norms.

'I had a momentary nervous breakdown. Couldn't take the strain. Cracked under pressure. Buckled under it. Do you need more phrases like this? I'm sure I can think of some more, once I recover from Junaid-bhai's gentle touch.' They were silent and after a few moments, I continued. 'I felt that my head was about to explode. I don't know why you people distrust me so much. You know full well that if I go back to where I came from, I'll either spend the rest of my life in jail or I'll be shot. Despite knowing that, you treat me like a prisoner. I can't go for a walk. My bedroom window has a burglar alarm so that I can't even open it. I can't make phone calls. I can't....' my words came out quick and fast in a tumble and even I started to feel sorry for myself. My eyes turned watery. However, they seemed to have little effect on Ayub and company.

'Poor Ritwik, he's a bird in a gilded cage, with due respects to the bird and the gilded cage.' Ayub had regained his mocking tone once again. I assumed that the *audi alteram partem* phase was over.

'The point I'm trying to make is that I tried to run away not because I am a double agent, but because I've had enough. I just had enough!' My voice rose to a high pitch and it trembled a bit. I started to feel much better, despite the throbbing in my head.

'That it? That's why you punched me on my nose and tried to flee?'

'Yes of course. That's it.'

Ayub took a deep breath and said, 'Fine. I'll accept that. You've been under a lot of pressure. You cracked under that pressure. It could happen to anyone. Hell, it could happen to me, couldn't it? I could have a nervous breakdown at this moment and might want to punch you on the nose and try to run away. And Junaid-bhai will have to try and stop me. Most probably Junaid-bhai won't stop me because his instructions are to keep you alive and secure, first and foremost. He is not meant to keep me secure or in his custody. He'll try and protect me if I am in danger, but that's secondary to keeping you secure and safe, do you follow me? In other words, if I were to just punch you and leave, I might easily get away with it. Junaid might not even block my punch though he can move faster than any other man I've known. He won't block my punch because it might hurt me. Junaid-bhai won't care if I punch you on the nose, because he knows that it won't kill you. He won't care that you might be in more pain or that your nose might bleed, as long as you are alive and in our custody. Do you follow me?'

'I don't see what you are getting at, Ayub?' I told him as crossly as I could.

'You don't, do you? Never mind that. Tell me about the Intelligence Assessment Group. Quite a cosy little group, isn't it?'

'I told you guys everything about the IAG when I was debriefed. What more do you want to do?' I was angry and irritated and made no effort to hide my feelings.

'Around fifty of you, from all over the world, working out of this small nook within the foreign office. A miniature version of the United Nations, isn't it?'

'Not exactly. It's more like NATO, with intelligence professionals from all over the world rather than just from both sides of the Atlantic. All those in the IAG are either military professionals or career spies like me.'

'Who's Josephine? She's not a military professional, is she?'

'Josephine? Josephine? Who's Josephine? I don't know any Josephine.'

'Josephine Delcour? *Vous connais*?'

'Oh! Jo! Yes of course, I know Jo. We all know Jo. She's one of the admin assistants.'

'She sleeps with General West, doesn't she?'

I was silent for a while. After a pause, I asked quietly 'And how did you know that?'

'Apparently it's common knowledge.'

'How remarkable!'

'Actually we know quite a bit about the IAG.' Ayub was silent for a second and then he asked fiercely, 'And why shouldn't we? The IAG spies on us, using clever men like you. We in turn spy on the IAG. Do you see anything wrong about that?'

'Not at all! So, you have someone inside who told you that Jo sleeps with General West?'

'Actually Jo told us that. She told us she was doing that to get access to information to pass onto us, provided we pay her well, which we did and still do.'

'The bitch!' I exclaimed.

'It was Josephine who told us about your predicament. She told us that you had a drinking problem and that you had your fingers in the till.'

'Now how could she have known that? My drinking problem, everyone knew about that. But very few people knew that I had, how shall I put it, taken some office cash for my personal use with every intention of putting it back.'

'Did General West know?'

'But of course. He is my, no, was my boss. He was the one who gave me two weeks to put the money back or face imprisonment.'

'And he sleeps with Josephine. That's how Josephine knew.'

'The bastard!' I exploded. 'I'll never again trust a man who has a wife or a mistress.'

'Like hell you won't. You guys knew that Josephine was selling whatever secrets she could lay hands on. She had a very expensive lifestyle. Holidays every two months, business class travel when on vacation, five star hotels, and who was paying for all that?'

'You tell me.'

'We were paying for it. We still are paying for it. And did General West know about that? Of course he did.'

'How do you know that General West knows about Josephine? If he did, he wouldn't be sleeping with her. She would be in jail by now.'

'She ought to be in jail, but she's not. And that's because '

'But how do you know all this? You are only guessing. You are guessing that because she has expensive tastes. General West and the others are bound to know that she has sold out. For god's sake, lots of people with low incomes have expensive tastes and don't necessarily fall under suspicion. Maybe they have an inheritance. Or maybe they married someone rich and got divorced. That's one way of making money.'

'Maybe we have someone else on the inside. Someone other than Josephine.' Here Ayub's voice became so, so smooth, the voice of a man who had controlled his anger for very long, one who was extremely tired of playing games. 'Someone who told us all along that Josephine was caught a year ago, that General West forced her to turn around, that you guys were using Josephine to send us information you wanted us to have, usually useless, though once in a while we did get something that we had some use for. But our inside source had told us that one day we would receive something that looks very useful, but would actually be a bomb disguised as a toy, meant to set us off the wrong path.'

'Well, if you have someone big on the inside, you won't need to worry,' I tried to make my voice sound casual, as if I didn't care, as if it didn't make a difference 'You will know when Josephine gives you a bomb disguised as a toy.'

'But Josephine has just given us a bomb disguised as a toy!' Ayub's voice was harsh, the smoothness totally gone. 'We used to wonder when the parcel would come along. We used to wonder when she would give us that one big thing that would explode in our faces.'

'She has given you a bomb disguised as a toy?' I tried to speak as normally as possible, even though my mouth had gone dry.

'Yes, she did. And it's you!'

'Me. Of course not! It's not me. It can't be me. I know that. I would know that, wouldn't I?' My voice cracked with the tension and effort.

'Listen, you poor puppy, listen while you still can. We've known all along that Josephine had been caught a year ago and that your people were planning to send us a sweet, perfumed, pink box full of explosive shit through her. A bomb disguised as a carrot. A bomb in an ice cream box. A toy. A soft toy. Put in whatever way you like. Nine months ago, she started to sleep around with General West. At least, she started spending a lot of time sitting around in his office, giggling away to glory and then they would leave together at the same time. She also started to give us more information than ever, saying she was getting it out of General West. We had to double her pay, though we knew she had been turned. Six months ago, you developed your drinking problems, right? You started to drink and gamble and Josephine started to tell us all about it. But we knew that you were a plant. We always knew that.'

'I see. And if you knew this all along, why house me with Junaid-bhai and his wife, why?' I wanted to say 'Junaid-bhai and his pretty young wife' just to irritate Junaid, but the very thought of Nilofer brought an ache to my heart and so I let it pass. 'Why take the trouble of feeding me for almost two weeks, if you always knew I was a traitor? Why pretend that you wanted to send me to Pakistan? Heck, you even booked my tickets! Why put that young man through the grill, forcing him to agree to carry a forged passport to Islamabad and present it to immigration there, just before I did?'

'Ritwik, we were indeed planning to send you to Islamabad. If there hadn't been a change of plan in the morning, you would be boarding your flight by now!'

'I don't understand. Why take so much trouble over me and send me to Pakistan if you thought I was a traitor?'

'Why? Because if we had bumped you off just after you defected, General West and General Qayyum would have figured out that we have someone else on the inside. Someone big. Someone who knew the whole plan. Only a handful of people in the IAG know that Josephine was a spy who has been turned and is now a double agent working for the IAG. Even fewer know that you are a plant. We thought it worth our while to play along for a while in order to protect our asset in the IAG. Our asset who warned us about you even before you landed.'

'I see. I see.' I wet my parched lips with my tongue and asked, 'What if your high-level asset is a traitor to your cause? What if he is playing a game and wants to discredit me? What if he is the double agent and I am the real McCoy?'

'Give us some credit, Ritwik. We might not be as clever as you are, but we are capable of making reasonable assessments. We see for ourselves the amount and nature of intelligence you have brought with you, we—'

'For heaven's sake, if only you would send me to Afghanistan, I can prove my worth.' I was shouting by then and my face was entirely red. 'If only you bastards would let me talk to people like Karim and Jabbar, I could show you which side I am on. Why can't you send me to Afghanistan and give me a month to show some results? I agree I haven't brought much stuff with me. But hey! What do you have to lose?'

They were all silent for a while. Then Ayub spoke. 'You know, Ritwik, you are so sloppy. You didn't even question us when we told you that we had accidentally found out your predicament. The story we gave you, that one of the Pakistanis working at the IAG told his wife that you are a drunken lout and she passed on the message to her brother who is a sympathiser, that story is very basic, isn't it? We didn't try to spin a better yarn. Didn't think it would be worth the bother because you were a plant who was all set to latch on to us. You didn't even want to know the name of the man who discussed you with his wife.'

'Of course I knew that was just a story. Look, I didn't question you because I didn't expect to be told who your source was. I mean, why would you tell me that?'

'Never mind that, Ritwik, I still have some good news for you. I was saving it up for the last.'

I looked surprised. 'What's the good news? That your asset in the IAG, the senior one, not Josephine, has asked you to buy me a drink for old time's sake? Maybe you'll let me have one of my bottles of Old Monk? Maybe all three of them? Just before you bump me off?'

'Now, now, don't jump to such hasty conclusions, Ritwik. What makes you think that…'

'Tell me,' I said, my voice low but urgent, 'Has this asset given you any information of any value? Maybe he was giving you low level semi-useless information until now in the hope of winning your trust. After I defected, he decided to discredit me. Maybe now he has given you something more of value to gain your trust. But I'm sure that valuable stuff is very recent. Tell me. No, don't tell me. Think it over first. Maybe.'

'Ritwik, Ritwik, my dear Ritwik, shall I promise you something? You won't die today! And you won't die tomorrow. Isn't that something? Whatever you do, you will be alive until midnight tomorrow? How does that sound? Do you feel better?'

I took a deep breath and said, 'Thanks a ton, Ayub. That's definitely cheerful news. Yes, I am feeling much better now. Can you get me a hot chocolate as well? I haven't eaten anything since this morning. We were supposed to grab some breakfast at Heathrow, weren't we?'

# 14

WE WERE SEATED AROUND THE dining table, the remnants of our breakfast all around us. 'I hope this isn't my last meal,' I said. 'I would rather say goodbye after dinner. There is something morbid about dying after a breakfast, even if it is a very satisfactory one.'

'Any other demands?' Ayub asked me with a smile.

'Yes, I would like some fresh underwear. And a good suit. I hate the idea of dying in dirty underwear or in these cheap clothes!'

'Fine. I promise. If we decide to kill you, I'll make sure that it's only after a decent dinner and you'll be wearing a Saville Row suit with some fresh underwear. The sort that smells of roses.'

'Thanks, Ayub. That's a big load off my mind,' I said as I drained the last of my coffee.

'Do you want to live, Ritwik?' Ayub asked me.

'No, not particularly. I am almost fifty. I don't have a family. There's no one waiting for me anywhere. I don't really care if I am killed. And that's god's honest truth.'

'Come on, Ritwik, every living being is programmed to fight for its survival. Why should you be any different? Isn't there anything you can tell us, in return for which, I could let you live?'

'You mean, is there anything I can tell you in the hope of saving my skin, after which Junaid will send me off to meet my maker?'

Ayub chuckled softly. 'Why do you think we offloaded you from that SUV today morning?'

'You tell me?' I challenged Ayub, staring him resolutely in the eye.

'Didn't I say I have some good news for you?'

I took a deep breath and said, 'Maybe you could get to the point, Ayub?'

Ayub didn't reply. Instead he looked at his plate and toyed with an egg spoon that was stained with pale yellow yolk. Munir looked annoyed. Junaid looked bored. Without looking up Ayub said, 'Last evening, our asset in the IAG found out that you are in possession of a piece of information that we would like to have. It was an accidental discovery. More importantly, it's information which you aren't expected to have. If you let us have this information, we could let you live.'

'You are talking in riddles, Ayub,' I said as tartly as I could.

'You are in Project A, aren't you?'

'What's Project A?' I asked innocently. Ayub nodded to Junaid in response and looked down once more. Junaid quickly got up and with his usual efficiency administered a stinging slap to my left cheek. A drop of blood made an appearance from the left corner of my mouth.

'You are in Project A, Project Amu Darya,' Ayub repeated without looking at me. I did not reply. 'In case you have forgotten, Project A has a glorious aim – to find out where Sheikh bin Laden and Mullah Omar are. Isn't that right?'

'If that's Project A and I am in Project A, what am I doing in London?' I asked Ayub. Once again Ayub nodded and I received another blow on my right cheek. A few drops of blood slowly seeped out of the other side of my mouth. It was a bit theatrical, though painful. Junaid definitely knew how to administer his blows, without overdoing them. I resolved to let my pride take a hit rather than my body, especially my once chubby and now hollow cheeks.

'You are here because you hoped to be sent to Afghanistan and win our trust there. You hoped, and your handlers hoped, that you would lead them to Sheikh bin Laden and Mullah Omar. Because that's what Project Amu Darya is all about. To capture two very clever and intelligent men who have outwitted the Americans and their lackeys for so many years. Despite having so many men and resources and technologies at their disposal, Allah's enemies have not been able to get anywhere near Sheikh bin Laden and Mullah Omar. And you, Ritwik Kumar, you thought that you could do what the Yanks haven't been able to do. Am I right now?'

I gave a shrug and mumbled, 'Maybe.'

'Louder. I can't hear you.'

'Maybe,' I said coherently, but not really louder.

'Maybe,' Munir repeated and laughed. Ayub smirked. Junaid had an amused look in his eyes, but he didn't laugh.

'Maybe? Well, that's a good start,' said Ayub. 'So you are in Project A and that's why you are here. Now, what's Project B?'

I remained silent, not having the guts to say that I didn't know. I looked down at my feet. 'Project B or Project Bahawalpur is to purge the ISI of all so-called pro-Taliban members,' Ayub informed me solemnly. Munir inhaled loudly enough for me to notice, despite the pain I was in. Ayub glared at him and he too looked down. I smiled inwardly. I was not the only guy in that room who was being bullied. Ayub had told nothing much to Munir and probably even less to Junaid! If this was how he ran his team, it was bound to be not too high on team spirit. On the other hand, if Munir or Junaid got caught, there was precious little they could tell anyone for they knew very little.

'And how has your General West been executing Project B? He plans to enter into a deal with a senior ISI officer, someone who commands loyalty among a sizeable section of the ISI. And what is the deal to be? In exchange for pointing their dirty fingers at those in the organisation who are loyal to their salt, rather than to green dollar bills, this Judas will be made head of the ISI and his people will receive promotions and money aplenty. The ones who don't sell out to the United States will be jailed or exiled or killed. That's Project B and General West has been at it for many months.

'We know that he or his representatives have had meetings with various senior officers, but so far, no one has been willing to betray his comrades. Mind you, there are many who know fully well where my loyalties lie and don't take my side. They may want to rid Pakistan of the Taliban, but very few of them will point fingers at me in the presence of an American and say, "Here, Master, this man Ayub Afridi, he is not loyal to your people. He is loyal to Islam. Kill him." No, sir, not many people in my firm will do that.'

'I know nothing about this Project B,' I told Ayub firmly.

Ayub ignored me and continued, 'However, there are bound to be a few people who are willing to worship the great Satan. We know that there are a few. General West and his people are talking to them. Our asset inside the IAG tells us that General West is very close to reaching a deal with one man, a senior Pathan officer in the firm, a man who comes from a very prominent Pathan tribe. However, we don't know who this officer is and where in London he has been put up.'

'I see. I see.'

'What do you see, Ritwik?' Ayub asked me.

'I can see how all of this is important to you. I guess once you find out who that officer is, you will kill him?'

'You are a clever man, Ritwik, I always knew that. But today you have outdone yourself. I wonder how you managed to deduce that? Are you sure you did a B.A. in Persian from JNU and not software engineering at one of your famous ITTs?'

'It's actually an IIT, but never mind, I couldn't do Math to save my own life. No, Persian is what I studied. But sarcasm doesn't become you, Ayub.'

'We will kill the bastard who is planning to help General West in his Project Bahawalpur just so that he can become head of the firm. I am a Pathan as well and if there is anything I hate, it is a Pathan who betrays his brother.'

'Best of luck then. I hope you manage to find this individual and kill him before he identifies to General West a vermin like you.'

'How dare you call Ayub-Bhai names like that?' Munir screamed. 'Junaid-bhai, teach him a lesson.' Both Ayub and Junaid ignored him.

'Ritwik, you are right now under the control of a vermin. If you can give the vermin the information he requires, you will live. If not, you will die.'

'What makes you think I have that information? Didn't your asset tell you that I was in Project A. If you know anything about General West, you would know that he is so paranoid and secretive that there is no way the same individual will work on more than one thing at a time. Everything on a-need-to-know-basis, that's General West's motto.'

'I know, Ritwik, I know. But sometime last October, that's October 2009, General West asked you to accompany him to a meeting with an ISI officer. Who was it? What was his name?'

'I don't remember a thing.'

'We can easily make you remember things, Ritwik,' Munir warned me.

'Munir-bhai, do you remember testing him when he got here first?' Ayub asked Munir who fell silent. He then turned to me and said, 'Ritwik, this is what we know. General West took you with him to a meeting with an ISI officer. The reason he took you along was because this ISI officer had with him a few of his underlings and he has a habit of speaking with them in rapid-fire Pushtu; General West thought that if you were around, you could later tell him what they were speaking. More importantly, General West wanted you to tell him if you thought the ISI officer he was meeting was lying. Apparently General West has a very high opinion of your ability to assess body language. This was the main reason why he took you along. You are not a fluent Pushtu speaker anyway.'

'I don't remember a thing,' I repeated.

'You just met that man once. Apparently you told General West that he is the genuine article. After that General West has been negotiating with him and with a few others. However, matters have progressed rather well with that particular officer. General West is now all set to reach final agreement with that traitor. And so, all I want from you is the name of that officer.'

I took a deep breath, swallowed and said, 'Let's assume all of this is true. I am not saying it is, but let's assume it is true, how will you find this officer? He could be in any one of the hundreds of safe-houses that MI6 has in and around London, which the IAG borrows from time to time. If General West is close to signing an agreement with this man, how will you find him before he hands over to General West a list of people like you in the ISI? What's the point of asking me for—'

'This is what General West was heard to say last evening. "I expect to reach a deal with the man I've been talking to. I wish Ritwik were here now instead of trying to worm his way in with those bastards. He was with me when I met him for the first time last October. In fact, Ritwik and I met him for the first time in the same safe-house where he has been put up for this round as well".'

'I thought your asset is very high level. Can't he tell you who this ISI officer is? Or doesn't General West trust him?'

'General West, clever bastard that he is, doesn't tell anyone anything, unless it is absolutely necessary. Last evening, he got slightly carried away because he is so close to a deal and he was feeling so euphoric. Also, all the people in that room knew that you are a plant and not a defector.'

We were all silent for a bit. Then Ayub said, 'Never mind all that. You have the information we need. You only need to tell us.'

They all looked at me expectantly. 'And what happens after I tell you, assuming I have this information?'

'Ritwik, you know how difficult it is to dispose of a dead body in this country. It is not like Afghanistan where as Kipling said, people don't make much of a fuss about a few bodies here or there. Hell, this is not even like India or Pakistan where you can, for a price, dispose of a few bodies. If we kill you, what would we do with your dead body? We could take it out at night and throw it into the Thames, but dead bodies always surface. We could bury you in the garden here, but some day someone will dig up the garden and find a few skeletons. On the other hand, if we let you walk away, what can you do? Can you go back to General West and tell him that you compromised his most important operation? No, you can't. So, we have nothing to fear from you once you tell us the name of this bastard and the details of the safe-house where you met him last October.'

'You'll let me walk away?' I asked incredulously.

'Of course. With a British driving licence or maybe even a passport, if we can manage it. Forged of course, but a good forgery. It's in our interest that you shouldn't be caught. You can find a job somewhere, something low profile and lead a life not different from a million other Londoners.'

I was silent. I was about to say something and then changed my mind.

'Look at it from my point of view. I believe that the Taliban are our friends. Or rather, they ought to be Pakistan's friends. I believe that the Taliban have been forced to fight the Pakistani army at home because of the way we betrayed them in Afghanistan. I also believe that Pakistan should not turn fundamentalist. I only want Pakistan to use the Taliban in Afghanistan and Kashmir. I will want Pakistan to be friends with the Americans and the British once they leave

Afghanistan. Once we win this round and I am sure that we will, it will be business as usual. I could be back in London as Pakistan's ambassador to the United Kingdom. If at that time your skeleton surfaces somewhere and it is found that I had a hand in killing you, it won't look very nice, will it? These Brits, you know them as well as I do, they are sticklers for matters like this. They are going to make a hue and cry and I don't want all that. In short, once you tell us what you know, I have every reason for letting you live and no reason to have you dead.'

I looked at Junaid. He had his mouth slightly open, a slightly expectant look on his face. Unlike Ayub, Junaid most probably hoped that I would tell them nothing and he could beat it out of me.

'Please indulge me, Ayub, what if—'

'Actually I have very little time to indulge you, Ritwik. For all I know, your General West is right now reading a list of names, my name on top of the list, which this traitor and his clansmen have given him. Maybe General West is already barking orders to hit squads in Islamabad and Peshawar and Karachi and London and New York to round up five hundred or so ISI officers and put them in jail.'

'What if I give you the wrong name? What if I give you the name of the wrong person in the wrong safe-house?'

'I did think of it. To begin with, we have an idea which among us are likely to turn traitor. If you give us a name that doesn't fit the bill at all, you will have bought yourself an express ticket to hell. Even if the name you give us sounds plausible, we will do our own checks. Finally, when we catch this man, we won't just kill him. We will have a chat with him. We will search him and his belongings. We will know whether we have caught a traitor or an innocent. And of course, you will be with Junaid till we are sure that we have got the right man.'

'No, Ayub my friend. I can't do this. I just don't have the information. You see, your so-called asset in the IAG is leading you up the wrong trail. He is the double agent. I am real. I am a real defector. There is no Project As or Project Bs. It's all just made up by him. The IAG only analyses intelligence. It has no scheme to catch bin Laden or Mullah Omar. And it has no intention of trying to purge the ISI. For god's sake, do you think the Pakistani government will allow a foreign agency to purge the ISI?'

'Ritwik, I forgot to tell you something. Our asset managed to look into your personal file kept at that foreign office. Apparently, last year they held a training exercise where the trainees were taught to resist torture. Water boarding was one of the things the trainees were subjected to, in a mild form, so that you guys know what to expect. Do you remember all that, Ritwik? Or have you forgotten this as well?'

I was silent, though I could feel a lump rising in my throat; I swallowed hard.

'Apparently, you didn't do too well with the water boarding, Ritwik. Apparently you confessed that you are claustrophobic and for one who suffers from claustrophobia, water boarding can be lethal. Almost lethal.' Ayub smiled.

I continued to be silent, though a bigger lump clogged my throat.

'Does this bit of information make you change your mind, Ritwik?' Ayub asked me.

I opened my mouth to speak, but no words would form. So I shook my head, a trifle slowly.

# 15

I WAS ON A STRETCHER AND MY arms and legs were strapped to the sides. A stout rope had been wound over my chest, groin and thighs a few times and I knew that I didn't have a snowball's chance in hell of escaping. We were in the bathroom; Junaid and Munir lifted the stretcher and slowly lowered it into the bathtub.

'The feet ought to be a bit higher than the head, that's what the manual says,' Ayub told them. He then looked at me and said, 'I have never done this before. I wonder if there are any extra precautions I should take when doing this to one who is claustrophobic?'

My eyes were wide with fear and I wanted to scream.

'We are supposed to cover your face with a cloth and pour water over it.' Ayub patted the large aluminium watering can by his feet. 'When the water goes into your mouth and nostrils, it induces the feeling of drowning. We will stop pouring water when we think you can't take anymore. However, since you are claustrophobic, you might gag much faster than someone who isn't, and if your face is covered with a cloth, you might drown in your own vomit. Any ideas how I could prevent this from happening?'

'Ayub-bhai, I swear to you, I don't know anything. I just don't know. If you do this to me, I will tell you some name and you will just waste a lot of effort after that. It just isn't worth it, Ayub-bhai.' I tried to speak in as normal a voice as possible, but my words tripped over one another.

'And if you give me the wrong name, Ritwik-bhai, we will kill you. It doesn't matter what it costs me later to dispose of your body, but I will kill you. No, I won't let Junaid-bhai kill you. I will let Junaid-bhai beat you up first and then I will kill you. Myself. I won't even use a knife. I will kick you to death with my own feet. After Junaid-bhai has had his way with you, that is. In fact, we will all be a bit disappointed if you now give us the information we want. None of us has had the benefit of the training you received at the IAG last year. We would all like to see water boarding in action. So, just hang on and don't scream. This is a residential area.'

As Ayub laughed at his own joke, I wondered if I should scream. If I screamed loud enough, some of the neighbours were bound to hear me. On second thoughts, I realised Ayub was bound to have made sure that all neighbouring houses were occupied by his own people.

People like Junaid. A scream would earn me little more than a clout to my head.

'Ready?'

I kept my eyes screwed shut. I started to count backwards from hundred. Hundred, ninety-nine, ninety-eight, ninety-seven, ninety-six, ninety-five, ninety-four, ninety-three, ninety-two, ninety-one, ninety.

A large brown towel was placed over my face. I started to vigorously shake my head, but the towel still covered my face.

'You still have time to speak up. But once we start pouring water, if you open your mouth to speak, water will go into your mouth.

'Noooooooo!' I screamed, a cry of total panic and fear. However, moments later as water started to fall on the towel and trickled into my mouth and nostrils, I stopped. I held my breath for a while. I started to count once more. There was a time when I could hold my breath for two minutes. That was ancient history and even if I hadn't screamed, I doubt if I could have held my breath for more than hundred seconds. I counted up to sixty and stopped. The water showed no signs of stopping. Despite having held my breath, some more water went into my nostrils. Soon, it was a flood. There was water inside my throat, inside my ears and inside my mouth. How big was the watering can, I tried to recollect. How could the water last for so long? I strained at my restraints so much that I could feel my eyes bulge out. There was a hammering in my eardrums and I felt as if I was underwater with tonnes of pressure on top of me.

When the towel was taken off my face, I threw my up a mixture of water and some of the excellent breakfast they had given me earlier that day. Since I was in a near horizontal position, all that went up into the air landed on my face. 'Poor you,' I heard Ayub say, despite the clattering in my eardrums. Someone, I think it was Munir, threw a few mugs of water on my face and that washed away the mess I had spluttered on myself.

'Had enough?' Ayub asked me. Before I could respond, he informed me, 'We start again in five minutes.'

'Noooooooooooo! Please, nooooooooo!' I never knew I could beseech anyone so earnestly, not a hint of ego or even self-respect in my voice. 'Ayub-bhai, if I knew anything I would tell you. I have absolutely no idea, Ayub-bhai, please let me go,' I begged. I was cringing and begging in the most abject and submissive manner possible that even the most destitute beggar in Bombay or Karachi would have envied me. If only I weren't strapped to the stretcher, I would have fallen at Ayub's feet and possibly even kissed it.

'Please kill me, if you think I am lying,' I suggested in the meekest voice one could imagine. I could hear the sound of the watering can being filled with water.

'You are lying, but I have no intention of killing you.' Ayub had steel in his voice. 'Ritwik, can't you understand? We can go on indefinitely. Can you?'

'Junaid, towel on the face!'

'Noooooooo!' I screamed as before, but stopped as soon as the water hit me. This time the water fell more slowly. I held my breath as before, but could only count till fifty before my chest started to heave. The water crept in like an old enemy, seeking passages everywhere, finding a few barriers and easily overcoming them. I struggled against the rope that trussed me to that evil stretcher and against the straps that held my arms and legs in place. I tried to turn the stretcher to one side, but that didn't work. Just when I thought my eardrums were ready to burst and that I would die, the water stopped. The towel was taken off my face and three pairs of eyes waited for me to throw up as before. I didn't. No for almost a minute. Then when Ayub bent down and asked me, 'No more vomit left in you?' I threw up what was left inside me of my breakfast and it hit Ayub straight in his face.

'Is this how you repay me for giving you toast and eggs?' Ayub asked me in a half-amused, half-irritated voice.

'Ayub-bhai, I will tell you everything I know. Please get me out of here,' I spluttered.

'No, you tell me everything you know first and I will then get you out of here. The meeting you had last October, the one General West took you to, who was it with?' Junaid handed Ayub a handful of paper tissues and Ayub started to wipe the puke off his face as he talked to me.

'The meeting General West took me to last October, that meeting....'

'Yes, you poor idiot, that's the one. Have you lost your head? If you like, I can give you another dose of this treatment. Junaid-bhai, fill up the can once more, let's...'

'Wasim.'

'What did you say?'

'Wasim Hunsud.'

'Say that again.'

'It was with a man called Wasim Hunsud.'

'I know that bastard. This was the guy General West met last October?'

'Yes,' I whispered.

'Don't look so embarrassed, Ritwik. You did put up a fight. Now, all you need to do is to tell us which safe-house you had your meeting in.'

'It was at a place called Basingstoke. Off the M3. Get off the M3 at Junction 6. Drive up to the train station. A huge block of pink and green flats opposite the train station. Called Noble Court or something.'

'Pink and green? Sounds ghastly. And the flat number?'

'God knows. I don't remember. There were around a hundred flats.'

'You don't remember?'

'No. I really don't. No.'

'Junaid-bhai! Is the watering can full? Just make sure these straps are tight. I think—'

'Ayub-bhai, I swear I don't have a clue. If I did, I would tell you, wouldn't I?'

'I am sure you are right. However, this water treatment might remind you of flat numbers that your brain has forgotten. It is not that I don't believe you. I just—'

'It was flat 604, on the sixth floor.'

'Are you sure?'

'Yes, of course. It's the only safe-house we have in that building.'

'Are you sure you are not making this up?'

'I am sure Ayub-bhai. I am definite. I am not making this up. Please let me go.'

'And this is the only safe-house the IAG has in that building?'

'That's right Ayub-bhai.'

'Hmmmmm. Junaid-bhai.' My heart stopped working until Ayub said, 'Untie him. Put him back in his room.' My heart started beating again.

# 16

I STAYED MOTIONLESS IN BED for over an hour before I could gather enough strength and courage to move. I then got down on my knees and started to look for the mobile phone I had stuck under the bed using duct tape. It was almost entirely dark inside the room since the window had once again been boarded up and the bulb seemed to have been removed from the socket. A couple of rays of light entered the room through two pinprick holes in the window boarding. I ran my fingers all around the entire underside of my bed, but I found nothing. Nilofer had indicated that she would nip into my room as soon as I leave for the airport that morning and retrieve the mobile. However, I was sort of hoping that she wouldn't have done so, since we had never left the garage.

I went up to the window and looked through one of the two small holes. The snow had almost entirely melted. There were still a few small patches of white left in a few spots, but the rest of the garden was submerged in puddles of slushy water. It wouldn't be much fun walking on the pavements outside, but considering my current predicament, I wouldn't have minded it so much, if only I had the freedom to do so. I tried the door and as expected found that the room was locked from outside.

My disappointment was only accentuated by how awful I felt. I was pretty sure that I wouldn't want to bathe or go near running water of any sort for a while. I lay down on the bed with the intention of getting some rest before I made a plan. However, I dozed off and when I woke up, the two pinpricks of light had disappeared.

I went to the bathroom and took a leak. I felt thirsty. I knocked on the door. There was no response. I knocked again and Junaid opened my door.

'I need some water. And some food.'

'Ayub-bhai has told me not to give you anything to eat or drink till he gets here.'

'That's ridiculous. I told you everything you chaps wanted to know and now you deny me a glass of water?'

'We forced you to tell us. If you had volunteered, we would be treating you differently.' I retreated a couple of paces from Junaid who seemed to be relishing his role. 'Ayub-bhai will be here very soon.'

'What's the time?' I asked and looked over Junaid's shoulder at the large clock on the wall. 'Quarter to six. When will Ayub get here?'

'Seven o'clock.'

'And till then I will have nothing to eat or drink?'

'Maybe you will have nothing to eat or drink even after that. Now go back to your bed.'

'Can I have my shoes back?'

'Why would I have your shoes?'

'Before you took me to the bathroom for the water boarding, you had taken my shoes off. They must be in that bathroom. It's cold and I need them.'

'Can't you wait till Ayub-bhai returns?'

The door was shut in my face. There was nothing more to be done than to lie on my bed. I was mentally exhausted. I considered trying to rip out the window boarding and making a run for it. Would Junaid be able to outrun me? Undoubtedly, but wouldn't I be able to reach the gate and attract somebody's attention. If I managed to rip off the boarding and get out through the window, I had a fair chance of making it. But what were my chances of ripping out the boarding with my bare hands? I couldn't afford to make any noise when I did so. Junaid was most probably in the living room from where he could listen to every noise that I made in that room. If I made it to the gate ahead of Junaid, would Junaid shoot me down or would he chase me to catch me live? Most probably he would fire at my legs. Was there a fifty percent chance that there would be someone passing by the gate at that moment? No, it was winter, it was already dark and from what I had gleaned from Nilofer, the house was not on any main thoroughfare. The chances of someone walking past the gate when I made my hurried appearance wasn't very high.

I wondered if Nilofer knew of my predicament. How would she react I wondered. Would she like me better if she knew that I was not a fugitive from civilisation? Or would she rather I were a defector plain and simple?

I went to the toilet and opened the hot water tap. The water had obviously passed through the boiler and tasted horrible. I then tried the cold water which tasted much better. I drank the water slowly so that I wouldn't get stomach cramps. I felt much better. Was I imagining it or was someone opening the door? I came out of the toilet to find the door open and Ayub standing in the doorway.

'Fancy any dinner, Ritwik?' he asked me as the light from the living room streamed into my dark bedroom.

'I thought I was supposed to go to bed hungry. That's what Junaid-bhai led me to believe.'

'For chrissakes, what do you expect? He's part of al Qaeda. They're a nasty bunch.'

'I thought you were one of them.'

'Me, Ayub Afridi, a Pakistani diplomat? One of them? Now you are really insulting me. We just use them from time to time, my dear Ritwik. We don't identify with them. We are definitely not one of them. We had them bottled up in Afghanistan, occupied with so many minor and trivial matters when the Yanks decided to invade the damn place and mess up things for my country. With that our strategic depth went out of the window and our on-demand tribal militias turned against us. We might as well give up our claim to Kashmir without those tribal fighters on our side and a friendly Afghanistan behind us.'

'Are you going to let me off? After all, I have told you everything that you need to know.'

'Not so fast, Ritwik. We need to corroborate what you've told us, which as it happens is not hundred percent accurate. Not because of any fault of yours, mind you. I know that it's not easy to remember the number of a flat one visited a few months ago.'

I gave Ayub a quizzical look. 'You said it was flat 604, on the sixth floor. Actually it's flat 703 on the seventh floor.'

'How did you find out?'

'We have our sources.'

'It can't be Jo. She wouldn't know. It must be your other source. The high value one.'

'Indeed it is. Our man in the IAG, he told us that the only safe-house the IAG has in Basingstoke is flat 703, Noble Court. And there is someone staying there now. Three guards and a couple of drivers have been assigned to that flat.'

'There you go. At least you know that I was trying to tell you the truth.

'Not so fast. You might still be making it up. But our man inside seems to think you are telling the truth. We will act on the information you've given us.'

'When will you let me go? Remember, it wouldn't help you at all if my dead body were to turn up somewhere in a few years' time when you are all set to become the Pakistani ambassador to the UK or to the United Nations.'

'True, but once we are sure that you have put us on the right track, we'll let you go. We do know that Wasim Hunsud is the sort of man who would consider a deal with

General West. He does have a following within the firm. He could possibly get a hundred odd officers to work with him in helping the Yankees purge the ISI. He has been making various trips to the UK and the US under one pretext or the other, without a really good enough excuse. Yes, it all sort of adds up.'

'So, let me off. Give me back my shoes, some dinner and let me go.' I was tempted to add, 'and let Nilofer go with me,' but I desisted.

'Hold your horses, Ritwik. You will have to spend another couple of days with us here. And we might have some more questions for you.'

'What questions?'

'Such as how do we gain access to that Flat 703? Our man only knows that Flat 703 is a safe-house. He has no idea about its layout, its—'

'As if I remember all that!'

'You might have to remember, Ritwik-bhai. You might have to. In case we decide to go in there. In the meantime, why don't we have some dinner? I'm sure Junaid-bhai's wife has concocted something tasty, as usual.'

'Can I have my shoes back please? It is very cold to be not wearing shoes.'

I got my shoes back after which Ayub, Junaid and I had our dinner in silence. Towards the end of the meal, Ayub said, 'From early tomorrow morning, the life of anyone in the firm associated with Wasim Hunsud is forfeit. By tomorrow afternoon, we expect to have killed at least fifty of his supporters.'

I shuddered and said, 'Now if I ever go back to General West or the IAG, my life will be forfeit.'

Ayub laughed at that and Junaid joined him.

I went back to my room, which was pitch dark and lay down on the bed. The door was once again locked from outside. I was exhausted and drained, but I knew that I wouldn't be able to sleep. I guess I was too exhausted to sleep. I wished I could speak to Nilofer, maybe touch her on her cheeks. I willed Nilofer to come to me. They say that if you want something desperately enough, you get it. One moment I was thinking of Nilofer and wishing I was with her. In another moment, I felt the door open softly and someone enter. It was not the firm click of Ayub's shoes or the heavy tread of Junaid's. Even before the person entered, I knew that it was Nilofer.

'I'm here,' I said very quietly in the darkness. A moment later, she was in my arms. She smelt and felt exactly as I had imagined her to smell and feel like. After a few seconds, I realised that Nilofer was sobbing.

'Hush my dear, don't cry. You are with me now.'

'I'm not crying,' she managed to say amidst her sobs.

'Are you okay? Have you had dinner?'

'Yes. Yes.'

We were both silent for a bit. Then she said, 'My husband was saying they wouldn't give you any food to eat.' At that Nilofer burst into tears.

'Don't cry now,' I said once more, as bravely as I could, though I didn't feel particularly brave. 'It's nothing. They did give me dinner. It's all coming to an end. I'll be free from here soon. Once I'm free, I'll come back for you. Okay?'

Amidst her sobs, Nilofer asked, 'Why is my husband so angry with you? I could hear you screaming. Did they beat you a lot?'

'No, they didn't beat me at all. It was nothing,' I said amidst a fresh outbreak of tears.

'Please tell me what's happening. I thought you are just a defector.' So the sweet girl had known that all along.

I was tempted to tell her everything, but for some reason held back. Instead of saying, 'I am not a defector. I am actually a double agent. I came here to plant some disinformation,' I said, 'There is some misunderstanding with Ayub-bhai and your husband. They think I have more information than what I've told them. We'll sort it out pretty soon, don't you worry.'

Since Nilofer kept sobbing, I asked her, 'Do you think they will notice that you are missing? If they ever find out, what excuse can you possibly give?'

'I don't know. I don't care. I will say I came here to replace the bed sheet or something.'

I laughed at such naivety and said, 'Darling, you ought to have brought a replacement bedsheet with you. But never mind. Where are they right now?'

'They are in the garage talking to someone over the phone. I think, to someone in Pakistan.'

'How do you know it is to Pakistan?'

'I don't know. I just assumed.'

I laughed at that. 'Maybe it is to someone in London?'

Nilofer laughed as well. 'Maybe. Let's run away. We'll make it. If you stay here, they'll kill you.'

'I can't, my darling. Not yet anyway.'

'Why not? Please tell me. I deserve to know.'

Once again, I was tempted to tell her everything, but for some reason I did not. 'Take my word for it. It'll all come to a close very soon. Very, very soon. Much sooner than you think.'

'I don't believe you,' she said. 'I have a feeling that something terrible is going to happen to you.'

'I'll be fine. I am worried about you. Maybe you should go back. If they ever find out, you'll be in big trouble. Isn't there a camera in the living room which is pointed at this door?'

'Don't worry. They stopped monitoring that camera's live feed some time ago. I heard Ayub-bhai tell my husband the other day. They don't have enough people. They record the feed and check it randomly later. And these phone calls they make usually go on forever. Even if they catch me, I don't care. What can they do to me? What more can he do?' More sobs followed that made my heart break.

'It'll all be over soon.' I paused and told her in English, 'I love you.' Three words that are better expressed in English than in any other language. I switched back to Punjabi. 'Did I tell you before that I love you?'

'I love you,' Nilofer responded in English.

'I'll always love you.' I kissed her on her lips. I kissed her hair, her fingers and her cheeks. I kissed her neck, her nape and her eyebrows.

'I love you, love you, love you!'

Bang! My door was open and Ayub stood in the doorway. Behind him stood Munir and a man I had never seen before.

'Hello! Who do we have here? Who's this visitor?'

Nilofer started to leave the room, edging past the two men. Ayub grabbed her hand and pushed her against the wall. The stranger used his elbow to further pin Nilofer to the wall by her neck.

'Don't you dare touch her,' I said and put my fists up.

Ayub drew his Glock 17 as he let go of Nilofer who was still pinned to the wall by the other man. 'Go on,' he challenged me. 'Go on, make a single move and I'll blow your brains out. Maybe it won't be a bad thing for you. Once Junaid sees this, he'll most probably tear you both to pieces.'

The threat of unleashing Junaid on Nilofer, rather than the pistol in Ayub's hand, made me quiet. Nilofer herself stood there quietly. The man slowly took his elbow off her neck.

'We have around three minutes before Junaid comes here,' Ayub told us. 'Three minutes for you both to convince me that I should let you stay alive for the next twelve hours.'

# 17

'HOW LONG HAS THIS BEEN going on?' Ayub demanded of Nilofer and me.

I decided to be partially honest with him. They were bound to question Nilofer separately later on and it wouldn't go well for her if Ayub thought I was lying outright. 'Nilofer felt sorry for me the day I had a fight with Junaid. She came to give me some painkillers. That was it. Today, because she heard me screaming, she was upset. Once again she came here just to see that I was alright.'

'I guess she thought that a few hugs and kisses would make you feel better?'

'It was just a harmless hug.'

'Yes, just a harmless hug. We'd rather believe you than trust our eyes.' The stranger who said that took it on himself to punch me in the head. It was not a heavy blow, but my head throbbed. I would have enjoyed swinging one back in return, but Ayub had his pistol pointed at me. Plus, there was Nilofer to think of.

'I'd like to leave,' Nilofer said.

'Let you off so that you can call the police to rescue your boyfriend?' Ayub asked her politely. 'No lady, you must think of something better than that.'

'I think you should definitely go back to your room, but Munir-bhai will have to accompany you,' Ayub said gently. He then turned to me and said, 'Though I would like to, I'm not going to tell Junaid what happened. He'll want to kill both of you immediately and I doubt if I can stop him. This is of course conditional on you doing something more for us.'

'Tell me,' I said. I had no bloody choice. It was no longer just my neck on the line. I had dragged Nilofer into this. I had to do whatever it took to keep her alive.

'Our asset in the IAG tells us that three guards and two drivers have been assigned to Flat 703. Apparently all these men are from a particular rota, which you used extensively and so they know you and will recognise you on sight. We want to kill that traitor Wasim Hunsud first thing tomorrow. You help us with that, and we'll let you both live. If not, I'll tell Junaid what happened and see if God will have mercy on Nilofer. In my experience, God rarely intervenes in matters such as these, though I don't personally like the idea of killing a woman, just because she has been unfaithful.'

'And what happens after I help you? Why should you let

either of us live?' Tired of standing, I sat down on the bed.

'I've told you this before, Ritwik. A dead body is not an easy thing to dispose of in this country. Two dead bodies, boy that's double trouble!'

'Junaid will never forgive Nilofer.'

'He doesn't have to know. I'll let you both live. You will most probably go back to IAG and tell them what happened. They won't kill you, but you'll have to look for a new job. Once this operation is over, I'll go back to Pakistan and lie low for a bit. Most of Wasim Hunsud's men in the firm will be dead by tomorrow. The IAG won't know what's going on till it's too late. All loyal ISI officers in London and the rest of the UK will leave with me. Once the firm is in our hands and all foreign influence has been purged from Pakistan and Afghanistan, I will negotiate my return. On my own terms. I'll order Munir to let you go once my flight lands in Islamabad. Nilofer should escape from here when Junaid is away and join you when she can. Do we have a deal?'

Like hell, Ayub would not let me stay alive. There was no way he could return to London if I was alive. Not after what they had done to me. 'Do I have a choice?' I asked Ayub, a sense of déjà vu sweeping over me.

'Our plans are a bit fluid at the moment. Once we start killing off Wasim Hunsud's men in Pakistan, Wasim is going to be very upset. My sense is that he will leave the flat and drive off somewhere. Maybe, ask for another safe-house. If we are to wait outside this building, Noble Court, we should be able to ambush the car. But I don't want to kill the driver or any of the guards. That's where you come in.'

'Please don't forget that for all the drivers and guards working for the IAG, I am a defector. A dangerous man to be shot dead on sight. You guys have a better chance without me. I am—'

'For God's sake Ritwik, hold your horses. I don't expect Wasim's guards to give you a hug when they see you. But if handled right, your presence can give us an element of surprise we wouldn't have otherwise. I just want to avoid killing the guard or the driver. If you don't distract them, Junaid will have to spray everyone with bullets indiscriminately. That's something I want to avoid.'

It made sense to me that Ayub wouldn't want to kill any of the British guards or drivers. Kill a senior Pakistani intelligence office in the UK and you might get away with it. Kill a lowly guard or a driver who is British and is employed by Her Majesty and you can rest assured that someone or the other will pursue you for the rest of your life. Not to mention the fact that the accused would find no safe haven in any developed country anywhere in the world as long as he lived. Given Ayub's ambition, the last thing he would want was to be associated with the murder of a British national.

Munir came back to the bedroom. 'Where's Nilofer?' Ayub asked him.

'I left her alone. She'll stay quiet. She started to beg me not to kill Ritwik. I told her that as long as she behaved herself, Ritwik'll stay alive.'

Ayub was silent for a minute, then he nodded his head. 'And that goes for you too. You be a good boy and Nilofer stays healthy and well.'

I was about to ask if I had a choice, but stopped myself.

'We need to keep you under watch all the time, till tomorrow's job is done. Munir-bhai will share your bed with you tonight,' Ayub notified me with a smile. Munir looked as amused as Ayub and I gave them both a wide grin. 'I'll try not to snore. Let it not be said that Ritwik was a bad bedfellow the night before he was killed,' I said.

'Ritwik, my dear Ritwik, you might come out of this alive. Just do all that we ask you to do tomorrow. Okay?'

I nodded my head, hoping that Munir wouldn't snore in his sleep. My hopes were belied. Munir snored like a pig, almost as loudly as I normally do.

# 18

ALL RESIDENTS OF NOBLE COURT are provided with an access fob to enter the building. Once inside, a set of six elevators carry them up to their flats. Visitors, on the other hand, are expected to dial the flat number they are visiting using a set of buttons installed outside the main door. After talking to the visitor through the intercom, the flat's occupant can open the door for the visitor by pressing a button installed on the intercom, which releases the front door's lock for a few seconds. Noble Court has an underground car parking with designated slots for each flat. Very early that morning Ayub spent around thirty minutes questioning me about Noble Court and Flat 703. The plan he formulated was very simple, one which depended on speed and execution for success. I must admit that I was rather impressed with Ayub.

Ayub, Junaid and I drove out of Junaid's house that morning in a BMW that was driven by the same young man with shoulder-length hair. As usual, they made me sit on the floor blindfolded until they had driven some distance. I was tempted to tell them to cut the rigmarole, but that could have got Nilofer into more trouble and so I kept quiet. On the way, somewhere near Tower Hill, we stopped outside a newsagent and picked up a man in his thirties who looked very fit and athletic; he sported a French beard. I wasn't introduced to him though he stared at me with curiosity for a long time.

Soon we were on the M25 out of London and then on the M3 towards Basingstoke. On the way Ayub's mobile rang. The call lasted a few seconds. The news evidently was good for he smiled a lot, said very good a few times and chuckled once before he hung up. 'We've bagged six guys already,' he told the young man with the French beard.

The GPS in the car made us exit the M3 at Junction 6 and take the A339 into Basingstoke.

Noble Court was as pink and green and ghastly as I remembered it to be. Bang opposite the Basingstoke train station, the fifteen-storey block of flats towers above all other buildings in the vicinity. The building is surrounded by green lawns with signs asking people to stay off the grass. In one corner of the compound, there are a few parking slots for visitors. Visitor Parking Only For Two Hours, a sign proclaimed, ostensibly with the intention of preventing enterprising train commuters from parking there for free instead of in the railway station's Pay and Park area.

We were lucky since the driver managed to park the BMW in a corner slot from where we could see the building's entrance as well as the steps leading to the underground car park for residents. We sat in the car and waited. After sometime a private security guard with mud-splattered trousers came up to us and asked if we were waiting for someone.

'Yes, we are visiting a friend in Flat 102, but he is away. Gone to the supermarket. Have to wait for him to turn up and let us in,' Ayub impatiently tapped the back of the seat before him. The guard walked away.

We didn't stand out in that car park since most residents of Noble Court are foreigners, mainly Indian and Chinese IT engineers working in the various technology companies that dot Basingstoke's landscape, one reason why the foreign office chose to have a safe-house there. It is very common for tenants to occupy a Noble Court flat for just a few months and leave. Many companies had rented flats and turned them into guesthouses for their overseas employees who came to the UK for brief stints.

Ayub's mobile rang. 'We've bagged two more of those bastards. I wonder how Wasim is taking it.'

'He must be hopping mad,' French beard commented. 'If he isn't hopping mad, he isn't human and he deserves to win.' There were smiles all around, even Junaid smiled.

That's the way to do it, I reminded myself. Treat it as a game and you won't get hurt. I unsuccessfully tried to banish thoughts of Nilofer from my mind.

'There is no doubt that the bastard is hopping mad. I just hope Uncle can pull it off,' Ayub said. The plan was for

Ayub's asset in the IAG to call up General West in the morning and raise a hue and cry over the killings in Pakistan. He was to ask General West if the IAG was negotiating with Wasim Hunsud. Why else were Hunsud's men being targeted, he would ask General West. In light of the rapid extinction of so many Hunsud men, General West would be forced to admit the truth, that it was with Wasim Hunsud he was close to reaching a deal. Ayub's asset would then suggest that Wasim Hunsud be moved to a different safe-house, especially because I was at large and I had been to Flat 703 when General West had his first chat with Wasim Hunsud. Hopefully, a nervous Wasim himself would be asking for such a move.

Ayub's mobile phone rang. Ayub listened intently and then stuffed the phone back into his jacket's pocket. 'Yeah, they are going to move the bastard. He should be coming out soon.'

'I hope they haven't given him any additional guards.'

'We can handle up to three guards. What I really like about these Brit chaps is that even when they carry weapons, they don't really expect to use them. It's not the same as the States. If this were happening in Texas, you can be sure that the guard would have a pistol he has fired hundreds of times other than for official target practice and he will have the safety off. Hell, we'd need three times as many men to do this operation there.'

'Texas in the only place in the West I admire,' French beard said in general. 'Those bastards are always ready for a fight. I like that.'

We didn't have long to wait. The building's door opened and a middle-aged white man emerged carrying a suitcase.

'That's the driver,' I told the others in the car. 'His name's Victor, I think. And that's Henry. He's the guard.'

Like Victor, Henry had a suitcase as well.

'Just Henry or are there others?'

'Let's see.'

'Hmm, isn't that Wasim?' said Ayub as a South Asian man emerged behind Henry, carrying a flight bag.

'I think so. When General West and I met him last October, he didn't have a beard.'

'That's him, the bastard. I've met him a few times,' French beard said.

Behind Wasim came yet another South Asian man, though he was much younger than Wasim. He too had a bag with him. It was evident that Wasim Hunsud was leaving Flat 703 for good.

'Is he one of ours?' Ayub asked French beard.

'Yes, I think so. Must be the guard assigned to him. His face looks familiar. Must he go as well?'

'Am afraid so. We can never be sure how he'll react if we let him live.'

Once all four men had come outside, they started to walk, as briskly as their luggage and the slush on the ground would allow them, towards the entrance to the underground car park. Ayub poked me in the back. I quickly got out of the car and ran towards them, my hands held halfway up.

'Henry! Henry!'

Henry gave me an open-mouthed astonished look, something similar to how I'd look if my maternal grandmother who had died a few years ago suddenly reappeared while I was at work.

'Henry, I want to give myself up. I need your help. There are a few men after me, I think.' I sounded petrified and flustered, just as someone who had defected and was on the run could expected to be. 'I just want to give up,' I repeated, holding up my hands shoulder high.

'Ritwik!' Henry sounded shocked. But possibly because I was so evidently unarmed, they didn't look scared or upset. 'My dear old chap, we've all been looking for you. We thought you'd be dead by now,' Victor's ever-jovial voice declared. Neither of the men made any attempt to take out the firearm each had under his jacket, though both men put their suitcases down.

'I made a mistake. A stupid mistake. I've been on the run from the guys I went over to. They wouldn't let me leave. I knew we have a house here. If it's empty, I could stay inside for a few hours while you guys whistle for help.'

'Heck no, I'm not sure we can do that. We have people there. Important folks. We need to keep that flat secure.'

'These chaps look as if they are moving out. Can't you give me the flat keys and report it to HQ. Someone can come down and take me away. In handcuffs if need be. I have some explaining to do.'

'I'm sure you do, but I don't think I can do that,' Henry sounded hesitant. Victor looked at Henry's face and nodded.

'Look here, who is this?' Wasim found a voice. Henry and Victor ignored him.

'I have a couple of friends with me. They are in the car. They helped me escape and now they are in trouble as well. If only we could stay in the flat for a few hours, we'd be safe.' I looked at the BMW and waved my hand. Junaid and French beard got out of the car and slowly walked towards us. At their approach, Victor and Henry looked uncomfortable, very uncomfortable.

'All three of us are in this together.' I told Henry and Victor and threw up my hands. The discomfort displayed by Henry and Victor as a result of my very oriental display of fatalism and despair did not please Wasim. 'Who is he? Please ask him to go away,' he told the two men as he put his bag down.

'We're quite harmless. Totally harmless. As long as you do what we ask you to do,' French beard told the company at large as he drew out a Smith and Wesson and waved it at Henry and Victor. I did likewise. The Smith and Wesson I had with me did not have any ammunition, but it looked as deadly as the loaded one French beard had.

Wasim's guard put down the bag in his hand and started to unbutton his jacket. However, it was too late. In one quick motion, Junaid took out his berretta and shot the guard in his forehead. Another bullet went in between Wasim's eyes. He then fired two more shots each into Wasim and his Pakistani guard.

'Henry, Victor, we don't mean any harm. Please just don't move,' I said firmly as the two men stood there looking shocked.

Ayub got out of the car and came towards us. 'The bastard got what he was asking for. We need to take these suitcases and bags with us. I'll take—' Ayub never completed his sentence. A volley of highly accurate fire swept all around us. Junaid fell to the ground and so did French beard. Ayub pointed his Glock 17 this way and that, but had no idea where the bullets had come from. Henry and Victor had smiles on their faces. I took a quick look at Junaid and there was no doubt that he was as dead as a dodo.

'Ayub Afridi, throw down your weapon and put your hands up,' a booming voice told him from a hidden speaker.

Ayub hesitated. I didn't. I spun around and punched him full in the face, catching him just above his left eye. He could have still shot me, but the sight of ten heavily armed men wearing full body armour running towards him possibly slowed him down. Further Henry and Victor had drawn their weapons by then and were pointing them at Ayub. I still remember the pleasure I felt as my knuckles made contact with the soft flesh on Ayub's handsome face. The pain felt so good as I wrung my fingers and kicked Ayub's Glock 17 out of his hand. I then punched him once again on his face, this time catching him squarely on his nose. The crack of his small nose bone did not carry far, but I didn't mind. For good measure, I kicked him on his kneecap, the left one, forcing him to fall down on the muddy ground. I was heaving. I realised that I hated Ayub Afridi more than any other human being in the world, more than I had hated even Junaid. Unlike Junaid who acted out of his mistaken convictions and beliefs, Ayub had been cold-bloodedly using men like Junaid to get what he wanted.

Before I could do any further damage to Ayub, Henry walked over, forced him up by his collar and handcuffed him. With the help of one of the armed men who had come up to us by then, a limping Ayub was led away. Behind me I could see the BMW's young driver being handcuffed and led off from the car by a plainclothesman.

Someone patted me from behind and said in a mid-west accent, 'So it all went off according to plan, eh?'

'General West! It's so good to see you, sir!' I almost hugged General West, but desisted, knowing that the man from Ohio was not a man keen on public displays of affection.

'I expected them to stay far away and use a long distance rifle to knock them off. Why did they want to get in so close?' General West nodded to Wasim Hunsud's and his bodyguard's bodies. As usual, General West was dressed in a sober grey sweater, which made him look beefier than he was, and black trousers. His thinning hair, which had turned entirely grey, was combed with a side parting. The brogues he wore made him look a trifle shorter than his six feet two inches height.

'Ayub was petrified of the possibility that he might kill a Brit. He thought that any fire towards Wasim would draw return fire from the guard and he would have to fire back.'

'So they made you get in close?'

'They did indeed. In a way, Ayub turned out to be exactly as we had profiled him.'

'Ha! It was I who profiled him for you guys. Time I got some credit.' That was Faisal Yusuf, ISI's head for the UK, one of the chief brains behind the current operation. I hadn't noticed him as he walked over to us.

'I was a bit worried that once you told him about Wasim, he might think you were no longer required and give you a quick send-off,' General West said.

'Not a chance. Not after Rashid would have told him all that you told him,' Faisal said. A tall, thin man who bore an uncanny resemblance to Jinnah, Faisal took out a silver cigar case, opened it to reveal two rows of fat Havanas and put one between his lips. A silver lighter was used to light the cigar and he took a deep puff with a sigh of relief.

'Where is General Qayyum now?' I asked.

'He is General Qayyum no longer. An hour ago, the Pakistani army relieved General Qayyum of his position and title. Mr Rashid Qayyum is now under lock and key.'

'Where's Ayub?' Faisal asked. 'I want to have a word with the bastard. He is still my subordinate and I somehow feel responsible for him. He comes from a very good family, you know.'

'They've taken him away. You'll find him in one of the vans, I think.'

'General West,' I said urgently. 'General West, actually it didn't all go according to plan.'

'No, what didn't go according to plan?'

'There's a woman who needs rescuing. She's Junaid's wife and she's being held a hostage because she tried to help me and they found out. But it's not as simple as that. I need to brief you before we—'

'I see. So there's a woman involved, is there? There always is, in matters like this. That's how these things turn out. And are you involved with this woman Ritwik?'

'Yes, sir, I am. You see, sir, I've fallen in love with her.'

# 19

'AND I THOUGHT EVERYTHING had gone according to plan,' General West said thoughtfully after listening to what I had to say. 'So you didn't offer to help them kill Wasim Hunsud in return for your freedom and a lot of money?'

'No, it didn't come to that. They caught me talking to Nilofer. After that, I didn't have a choice, but to do what they asked me to do.'

'And they asked you to help distract Victor and Henry so that Junaid could finish them off?'

'Yes, sir, that's right.'

It took me another thirty minutes to explain everything to General West and make arrangements. Soon, we were in an unmarked van racing towards Mile End. The van was being driven by an ex special forces driver who seemed to think that the slush on the road created extra traction and that speed limits were strictly for wimps.

'Are you comfortable in that position?' General West asked Ayub who was sitting with his face almost stuck to the pole to which he was tightly handcuffed. My handiwork was displayed on his face in vivid technicolor. His left eye was totally black and there was blood all around his nose.

'I'm not going to complain, General West,' Ayub replied. 'A man in my position can't afford to. I have heard a lot about you. It is such an honour to meet you in person, though I would have preferred meeting you under different circumstances.'

'You would have preferred it if we had lost this round and Wasim Hunsud were still alive, you mean.'

Ayub looked confused for a bit. 'I still haven't understood why you allowed us to kill Wasim. Did you want him dead?'

'Actually yes. We also wanted you to start some intra-ISI blood-letting in Pakistan. According to my sources, so far fifteen men close to Wasim Hunsud have been killed by other ISI officers. Just to think that he had firmly rejected my offer to come over to my side so many times. Mind you, he was a diligent and obedient officer. Every time Faisal ordered him to London, he would turn up here on the dot. Pity he had to die.' I saw Ayub's knuckles go white as they tightened their grip on the pole he was handcuffed to.

'My congratulations, General. You were on to General Qayyum all along, weren't you? You were able to accomplish all this because of that.'

'That's right. Once we knew that General Qayyum was a traitor to his country, we decided to use him. We allowed him to know that Ritwik was being planted into the pro-Taliban community in London. We made him think that Ritwik's objective was to succeed in Project Amu Darya. Then just before Ritwik was to fly to Islamabad, we told him that Ritwik knew about Wasim Hunsud and Flat 703.'

'How did you know when Ritwik was to fly to Islamabad?'

'We had cottoned on to Bhaimeet Singh Travels some months ago. Yes, it was a good idea to use a small travel agency in Southall to buy your tickets and you always paid in cash, but then, when you buy too many tickets, that sort of stands out. So when Bhaimeet Singh purchased a ticket for Sajid Khan, and the real Sajid Khan was staying in Birmingham with a cousin and showed no signs of planning to travel, we knew that Ritwik would be travelling on his ticket.'

'General West, I am very, very impressed. You have been so much ahead of us.'

'Just as we knew that after you booked a ticket to Delhi from Lahore in Ritwik's name using Bhaimeet Singh Travels, Tiny Tim would send his goons to Ritwik's house to collect his money even before it was due. Just as we knew that you would be there to rescue Ritwik when Tiny Tim's goons went about their collection.'

Words failed Ayub. 'So Ritwik knew that we would be there to rescue him when he took on Bob and Eddie?'

Instead of replying, General West said, 'It was a smart move. Booking a Jet Airways ticket in Ritwik's name and getting Bhaimeet to post it to the wrong address, the address of one of Tiny Tim's men.'

'So Bhaimeet was co-operating with you all along, was he?

'Yes, unfortunately for you. It is easy for people like you to buy out small businesses like Bhaimeet's, but it is also easy to turn them around and get them to work for us once we confront them with the truth.'

'But I just don't understand why you went to all this trouble if you always knew that General Qayyum was on our side. Why didn't you just arrest him?'

'We didn't have real proof and the Pakistani government couldn't be persuaded to charge General Qayyum without real proof. He has diplomatic immunity after all. He was too senior for the Pakistani government to arrest on mere suspicion. He always spoke with you and other traitor ISI officers inside the Pakistani High Commission where we couldn't tap your conversations. Lots of ISI officers, even the ones working for us, knew who was loyal and who wasn't. However, very few of your colleagues were willing to go along with a cleanup operation. We had to start somewhere, get ISI officers to point fingers at the traitors in their midst who support the Taliban and cause the deaths of so many American and British and even Pakistani soldiers. Now that your men have killed so many of Wasim's men, and the killings will go on for a while, maybe things will change.'

'You still don't have real proof against General Qayyum, do you? It's still your word against his.'

'Well, it was General Qayyum who told you the correct

number of the flat where Wasim was staying. Ritwik didn't give you the right number. That sort of clinches the matter I'm afraid.'

'That was very clever.' Ayub sounded really impressed. 'But you still don't have a list.'

'Actually we have a few lists. Faisal has compiled one. Ambassador Zahir Junejo has compiled another. No, we don't have a shortage of lists. We just couldn't get ISI officers arrested in Pakistan or thrown out of the ISI even if we knew they were traitors. All that will change now that your men have shot dead fifteen odd ISI officers who had no intention of helping us in the first place.'

'You still don't know where bin Laden and Mullah Omar are.' I noticed that Ayub no longer used the pre-fix 'Sheikh' for bin Laden.

'No, we don't. We'd like to, but in my opinion, it is not critical. The al Qaeda and the Taliban are so decentralised that they have hundreds of bin Ladens and Mullah Omars within them. Of course, these two chaps are figureheads and it will look good if we can catch them, but it ranks very low on my list of priorities!'

'So, you got all that you really wanted? Except that you won't be able to date Josephine any more. Or send more false information through her. Her cover is blown, isn't it?'

'Rashid Qayyum blew Jo's cover immediately after we caught her a year ago and she agreed to turn a double-agent. It was then that we started suspecting Qayyum. Later our suspicions hardened into conviction. When Ritwik and I came up with this plan to have Ritwik defect to your side, we decided to use Jo, knowing fully well that any information she gave you would be treated as misinformation.'

'Good excuse for you to date her,' Ayub said, a polite smirk on his disfigured face.

'And why not? This job is meant to come with a few perks. Mind you, she has promised to keep visiting my wife at home. She's not a bad sort, though she has expensive habits. If Qayyum wasn't a traitor, she would have done some very useful work for us after she was turned.'

Ayub then turned to me and said, 'You really had me fooled. I never thought someone who is claustrophobic would go through a few water boarding sessions and still have the presence of mind to feed me with wrong information.'

'Ritwik gets claustrophobic pretty easily,' General West informed Ayub. 'Once he went caving with a few others, that's his hobby, caving, and they got trapped in an underwater cul-de-sac after a few rocks were dislodged. They were trapped there for fifteen hours before someone arrived to pull them out. Ritwik tells me that he started to feel terribly claustrophobic towards the end.'

'So that was another mis-feed, wasn't it? I only have General Qayyum to blame. He led me to believe that he was in your good books and you had full faith in him.'

'Dear me, did he say that? He did feed us some information, but we weren't really impressed with that. Though we didn't tell him so to his face.'

'You guys won. And, sir,' Ayub turned his face towards me and said, 'you will get the lady who you richly deserve. Munir is watching over Nilofer, but I'm sure she'll be alright.

I never had any intention of harming her. I won't deny that I had an agenda and that I was willing to use the Taliban to achieve my goals and what I feel are legitimate goals for my country. But it did break my heart to see the way Junaid treated his wife. I'm glad he's dead. Nilofer is all yours.'

'I hope you still have my three bottles of Old Monk. When all this is over, I want them back. You'll be in big trouble if those bottles go missing.'

'You'll get back your booze. You'll get Nilofer. You'll get everything that you deserve. You guys have been so clever. You chaps—'

General West didn't let Ayub complete his flattery. 'We'll be reaching Mile End soon. You'll have to tell us which way to turn.'

'But of course General West. Are you sure you don't want me to call Munir and tell him that we are on our way back and everything is alright? I could ask him to free Nilofer right away.'

'No,' General West said quickly before I could say anything. 'No, let's do it this way. Let's go in unannounced.'

'You still don't trust me, General,' Ayub muttered.

'Actually I don't,' General West retorted with a kind smile. I have seen General West shoot men dead with the same smile.

'Left and then the first right,' Ayub told the driver.

'Slow down a bit,' General West told the driver after we had turned left. He then turned to the SAS man sitting next to the driver and said, 'Ask them to overtake us.'

I curiously turned around to see Ayub's BMW drive up to our van and then overtake us. It was being driven by the young man with shoulder-length hair. There were three SAS men in the car and they were all heavily armed and wore full-body armour. 'We are told that the woman is being held hostage by just one man who only has a pistol. But don't take any chances. Get in quickly and if there is any resistance, shoot the man dead,' General West told the SAS man who sat in front and he relayed the instructions to his comrades in the BMW.

'I'm sure there is no need for all that, General West,' Ayub said mildly.

I was a bit annoyed with myself for not having noticed the BMW behind us. I guess I was so exhausted with what I had gone through and the fact that I was now in General West's hands.

'I want to stop some distance from the house,' General West told Ayub.

'Once you turn right, there's a petrol station. You could wait there if you like,' Ayub suggested.

'Good idea,' General West agreed. We didn't have to wait long. Hardly had we stopped inside the petrol station that the SAS man sitting next to the driver in front received a message. He then turned around and told us, 'They have taken the house. One man captured. He has been disarmed. The woman in the house is unharmed.'

'Fantastic,' I screamed with happiness and got a pat on the back from General West. I could only imagine Munir's reaction as two or three SAS men got out of that BMW and charged into the house. I smiled to myself.

We drove to the house and the van finally stopped in front of a very unremarkable detached house with a courtyard barely large enough to park a car. I felt somewhat weird. This was the place where I had lived, nay where I had been imprisoned for the better part of two weeks. And yet, I could not recognise it from outside. The courtyard was ringed by a wicket fence that was not more than four feet high, but which led to the much taller fence in the rear! To think that I had been imprisoned in such a run-of-the-mill house! The outer gate was ajar and the front door had been broken down. I got out of the van before anyone else could and rushed inside. I ran into the living room where Munir was sitting on a sofa, his right leg handcuffed to the leg of the sofa. I ignored him and went to the kitchen and then to the master bedroom. There was no sign of Nilofer.

'Where's the lady?' I asked the bemused SAS men.

'She's in that room,' they said and pointed me to my old bedroom. With a trembling heart, weak knees and wobbly legs, I went in.

# 20

NILOFER WAS SITTING ON THE bed with her face in her lap and her hands covering her ears. Her legs were under the bed, the heels pushed up against the underside of the bed. It was the closest she could get to a foetal position sitting on that bed, with her feet down. She was still covered in that miserable burkha.

I walked up to her, almost on tiptoe, patted her on her head and said, 'It's me, Nilofer. Nilofer, it's all over. I'm safe.' I spoke in Punjabi.

Nilofer lifted up her head and looked and me with those bright, round eyes of hers.

'He's dead. I'm sorry.'

'My husband?'

I nodded.

'And Ayub-bhai?'

'He's alive. He's in the van outside, handcuffed to a pole, an SAS man guarding him. He'll be in jail for a very long time, don't worry.'

Nilofer took a long breath, but remained silent, as if she couldn't believe all that I had told her. Finally she said, 'I was so worried. I thought I would never see you alive.'

'We'll go away from here. I'm going to stop doing the stuff that I've been doing for the last twenty-five years. I'll do something different. Maybe teach Persian somewhere. And we'll get married. You'll have a new life, I promise you.'

'This is all too sudden for me,' Nilofer said showing no signs of wanting to get up and hug me. I then realised that an SAS man was standing behind me.

'Can you please leave us alone for a bit?' I asked him. He hesitated for a bit and then said, 'I'll be just outside. Holler, if you need me.' With a grin, he left us alone.

'Please take that bloody thing off,' I said as soon as we were alone. Nilofer hesitated a bit and then removed the hideous black veil that covered her pretty face.

She was as beautiful as ever. I cupped her face with my hands. Nilofer started to sob. 'My dear, it is all over. Soon you'll realise that everything has changed. You'll never have to put up with so much abuse. You'll have everything you need. Everything money can buy, on the salary of a Persian teacher, that is,' I added with a smile.

'Where's Ayub-bhai?' Nilofer asked me again.

'In the van outside. He's handcuffed and those will stay on him for a long time, don't worry. He'll be in jail for the rest of his life, unless they decide to extradite him to Pakistan and execute him.'

General West rushed into the room. 'I thought that's enough privacy for you two lovebirds. Time to get to work, Ritwik. There's so much to be done.' General West had clipped a holster to his belt and his pistol, an old-fashioned Colt, stuck out of it. He then turned to Nilofer and asked, 'Is this the lady?'

'Nilofer, meet General West. He is my boss and he heads IAG where I work.'

Nilofer slowly lifted up her eyes and looked at General West. 'General, I owe my life to Nilofer. She kept me sane. If it hadn't been for her, I'd have gone nuts.'

'And here I was thinking everything was going according to plan! What would you have done if this lady weren't around? Didn't you sign up for all the shit that was dished out to you?' General West was at his gregarious best.

'Is there a place I can take her to, sir? She needs to leave this place at once. She shouldn't stay here for a moment longer than is necessary!' I announced.

'Ritwik, please calm down. Let the lady tell us what her wish is. Don't let Ritwik force you into doing anything you don't want to, my dear,' General West told Nilofer as he walked up to her, the Colt dangling from his waist.

'Are you sure you want to go with Ritwik?' General West asked Nilofer. 'He's not a bad guy, but I know quite a few of his dirty secrets. After you hear what I have to tell you about Ritwik, you can—' General West never completed what he was saying. Quick as a flash, Nilofer leaned over and grabbed the

Colt from General West's holster. I looked incredibly stupid and silly as Nilofer announced, 'Don't move. Both of you stay where you are. I'll shoot if you move.' Her voice was jerky and her hands even more so, but there was no mistaking the anger and hatred in her voice. And the hatred was directed not only towards General West, but also towards me!

'So, we were both mistaken, were we?' General West asked quietly.

'Yes, you idiots. You men! You are such stupid idiots!' She then turned to me and said, 'Each time you touched me, my skin crawled, you bastard.' I was dumbstruck.

'We both fell for you, didn't we?' General West said again. 'Tell me,' he asked Nilofer. 'How long have you worked for the al Qaeda?'

'The al Qaeda? I don't work for the al Qaeda. I work for...,' here Nilofer hesitated. Then her tone became assertive. 'I work for Pakistan. Just like Mr Ayub Afridi. We are both patriots. We want our country to be powerful and strong.'

'I see. So you want Pakistan to be strong. For that, you pretended to help Ritwik?'

'This irritating bastard.' I got a contemptuous look. 'If only he had made a single mobile call, he would have saved everyone so much trouble.'

'Oh! I don't know this. Did Ritwik have a mobile phone with which he could have made a phone call?' General West asked me.

I nodded my head miserably. 'Yes, she gave a mobile phone and called me. I didn't have time to brief you fully.'

'You just told me that the love of your life is in danger and we both rushed over here,' said General West, boiling with anger.

I looked as if the sky had fallen on me. 'If only you had used that phone to call General West and tell him that you were at Mile End, Ayub could have had you killed,' Nilofer said wistfully. 'I did tell you that our house was at Mile End, didn't I?'

'I don't understand,' General West shook his head. 'You could have killed him in any event. Why give him a mobile and wait for him to call me before killing him?'

'If we had killed this idiot for no reason, General Qayyum's cover would have been blown. You would have guessed that there was someone else in the IAG spying for us, someone other than Josephine. But if he called you from that mobile and was executed later, you'd think his call had been detected and got him killed as a result. You wouldn't have suspected General Qayyum.'

'I see.' General West continued to be politely curious.

'So we were all set to send him to Pakistan, just to ensure that General Qayyum did not fall under suspicion.'

'And would you have killed him immediately after he landed there?'

Nilofer shrugged her shoulders and said, 'I think they planned to send him on to Afghanistan and have him step on a landmine.' She gave me a scornful smile. I was too deeply upset to be able to respond.

We were silent for a few seconds. Nilofer finally broke the silence. 'Enough of this. I want you to ask the man outside to bring Mr Ayub Afridi inside. If either of you try anything, I'll kill you. I've got nothing to lose.'

'Actually, my dear, you have a lot to lose. If you fire a single shot with that Colt, and that pistol makes one hell of a lot of noise, the SAS man outside will come in and most probably blow your head off with his automatic rifle. If I were you, I'd try to escape on my own. Tie us both up and make a run for it through this window.' General West pointed to the window behind him from where the boarding had been removed.

'Maybe, I should martyr myself for the cause. And take you both with me before I get killed.' Nilofer's fingers tightened around the trigger. 'A dead general is a good enough trophy,' she added. I guess my value as a trophy wasn't very high or maybe Nilofer didn't regard me very highly, since she didn't mention me.

General West looked at me and took a deep breath. 'Go on, Ritwik. We have no choice. Just to think that we are faltering at the very end. It's all your bloody fault.'

I hesitated, still smarting from General West's criticism.

'Get Mr Afridi here. Or else I will kill you both,' Nilofer repeated.

'Why do you desperately want Ayub Afridi? Granted, he is a handsome man, but your husband is dead and you should be mourning for him and trying to save your skin.'

'I love him,' Nilofer told us with a vehemence I would not have believed if I hadn't seen it firsthand.

'What? You love Ayub Afridi? Is that why you did all this?' General West continued to prod.

'Yes. And for my country, Pakistan.'

'Aren't you a British national?'

'Yes, but I will always be a Pakistani. I will do anything for my country.'

'Tell me, as a good Muslim, wasn't it wrong to have been unfaithful to your husband? I assume you have been having an affair with Ayub Afridi.' General West sounded as if he was having a discussion with a neighbour in his native Ohio rather than one with an angry and nervous woman in a burkha, with a loaded Colt in her hand.

'That animal deserved nothing better. Mr Afridi is a gentleman.'

'You both believe that the Taliban are friends of Pakistan, don't you?'

'Of course. Are you going to call Mr Afridi in or shall I kill one of you?'

I gave Nilofer a shrug that was meant to convey my defeat and went over to the door, put my head out and shouted to the SAS man sitting on the sofa in the living room. 'Please ask them to bring that man in handcuffs to this room.' The SAS man hesitated. 'Right away,' I repeated loud enough for Nilofer to hear.

'How long have you been involved with Ayub?'

'Ever since I saw him for the first time.'

'And when was that?' It seemed that General West's curiosity knew no bounds.

'After my miserable husband turned religious and started working for the al Qaeda. I guess I should be grateful to you for killing him, though they won't be pleased.'

'They? Who's they?'

Nilofer sighed. 'Mr Afridi and others. They found my husband very useful.'

'Are there lots of others? How many men work for Ayub in London?'

'Never mind.' We could hear footsteps coming in.

'I don't want that soldier to come in,' Nilofer shouted at me in Punjabi.

I went outside once again, stuck my head out and told the two SAS men who were bringing in Ayub, 'We'll take it from here.' I nodded at Ayub who was limping and said, 'Come inside.'

Ayub wearily walked inside. His face had become even more swollen and his left eye was shut. I felt proud of myself.

'Oh my god!' Nilofer's anguish was genuine. 'What did they do to you?' she asked Ayub, who then looked up and saw that Nilofer had the Colt in her hand.

'How'd you manage this?' he asked and he quickly took the pistol, holding it with both his handcuffed hands, and waved it at us.

For a second Nilofer didn't reply as she continued to stare at Ayub's face, her mouth open. I still thought that she looked incredibly pretty.

'Did you know that if you hadn't played that game and allowed yourself and Ritwik to be caught by Ayub, Ritwik would have offered to help Ayub kill Wasim Hunsud for a large amount of money? That was our plan!' General West told them both.

'Nilofer, how could you do this to me?' I asked. 'I thought you loved me!' We were quite a combination, me and General West. I was still grief-stricken because of my betrayal and General West seemed to be only interested in having a long conversation with Ayub and Nilofer without a care whether they fled or not.

'If you had fallen for me, why didn't you tell me that you knew General Qayyum was on Ayub-bhai's side? That you wanted to be put through water boarding? Why didn't you tell me all that?' Nilofer questioned.

'I honestly don't know,' I admitted. I had indeed thought myself to be in love with Nilofer, but I hadn't given the game away. They had never found out that I knew that they knew I was a double agent.

'It was Ritwik who did this to my face.' Ayub told Nilofer. Nilofer was silent for a few seconds before she said with a note of anger, 'We'll make him pay for it, but first we need to open those handcuffs.'

'Never mind that. Do you have a phone?' Ayub asked Nilofer.

'Yes, of course.'

'I hope it has sufficient credit,' I put in. They ignored me.

'Call up the boys and tell them what happened. Tell them to stop killing Wasim Hunsud's men immediately. Tell them it was a sham, that Hunsud was a good man. Tell them that we were tricked into killing Hunsud's men in order to make us fight among ourselves and make us weak.' Ayub walked backwards, never taking his eyes off us and shut the door behind him.

Nilofer fished out a mobile phone from inside the folds of her burkha and started to dial. I wondered if she would ask Ayub whom to call, but she didn't. She definitely knew who to call in an emergency. She dialled a number and held the phone to her ear. After a while, she shook her head. 'Can't get through,' she told Ayub in Punjabi. 'Bad connection.'

'Shammy?'

Nilofer nodded.

'Try Mo.'

Nilofer dialled and held the phone to her ear once more. She shook her head after a few seconds.

'Try again. Keep trying.' The note of desperation was hard to miss in Ayub's voice.

Nilofer dialled again. A few seconds later she shook her head.

'Try the others. Keep trying,' Ayub told her, his mouth set in a grim line. I don't know if the grimness was more on account of the pain from his war wounds or his situation.

After another two attempts, Nilofer shook her head again.

'The SAS men outside must have jammed this area. I had told them to. You can make calls only if you do it on a particular frequency. You won't be able to do so from that phone,' General West gently told Ayub.

'Do you have a phone from which I can make a call?' Ayub asked General West.

'Yes, of course. I head the IAG, don't I? We have the latest in this sort of technology.'

'Well, then give it to me, man!' Ayub shouted. He was speaking in a hoarse voice.

General West ignored him. Instead he asked Nilofer, 'Have you heard of the Tantalus Test? You have failed it.'

Ayub pointed the pistol at General West and said, 'I'll count to three. If you don't take your phone out and keep it on the ground, I'll kill you.' He started to pull the trigger.

'A pity you haven't heard of the Tantalus Test!' General West repeated. 'Tantalus was a Greek king who angered the Gods. The Gods wanted to punish him. So they placed him—'

'You dumb fool! I will kill you and take your phone!' Ayub screamed at General West.

General West ignored him and continued, 'Tantalus was placed next to an unloaded Colt pistol. He grabbed it and tried to kill two men, a general and a spy. Tantalus paid for his mistake dearly.'

There was silence for a while. Then Ayub looked at his pistol with dismay and said in a very gruff voice, 'I don't believe you, you bastard.' He lifted the Colt, aimed it at General West and pulled the trigger. There was an empty click. Both General West and I took out our pistols from inside our jackets.

'Come inside quickly,' I hollered.

A second later, the SAS man was trying the door, which shook at its hinges.

'Should I open the door?' I asked General West.

'No, let them break it open,' he said. 'Not worth the risk. And it is not my house.' If I wanted to open the door, I'd have to walk past a distraught Ayub and a shocked Nilofer. If Ayub tried to grab my pistol, I'd have to shoot him.

The door fell in and three SAS men rushed in. 'Sir, are you alright?' they asked General West in unison.

'Yes, I am,' General West said. He walked over to Ayub and took the Colt pistol from him. Ayub didn't offer any resistance. I pocketed the mobile that Nilofer had in her hand. As I took the mobile, my fingers brushed against hers and an involuntary tremor shook me violently.

'I was in love with you till today morning,' I told Nilofer in a genuinely sad voice. 'You did a good job of fooling me.'

'Last night, after we were caught in this room, you were so upset. But then as you walked out with Munir, you walked out in front with Munir behind you. That's when I started to suspect you. Your face showed worry, but your gait didn't. It was a confident walk. Anyone who can walk with such confidence when there is a possibility of being lynched by her husband deserves an award for bravery. Later when Munir came back saying you had promised to behave yourself if they didn't harm me, I became really suspicious. Why on earth would anyone in your position, assuming you hated the Taliban and wanted to escape with me, rely on such a promise? Why wouldn't you call the police on the sly and ask them for help? And why would Munir leave you unsupervised? Of course, they didn't have enough people, but still. Then I thought back to all the other things you did. The day Junaid slapped you, you were sobbing so loudly that I could easily hear you in my room, through the wall. You could switch off the burglar alarm when you wanted to. Yesterday you told me that they had stopped live monitoring of the camera's feed. It seemed to be a very sensible thing to do. Just when I had been exposed, tortured and had every reason for trying to escape, you stop live monitoring of the camera's feed! It all just added up.'

'Am I glad you didn't tell her that we knew Rashid to be a double-crosser. You nearly did, didn't you?' General West asked me.

'Yes, sir. I mean, no, sir. I wouldn't have done that.'

'Like hell, you wouldn't.' He was right. I had almost blown the whole operation. I was angry more at myself. How could I have been so gullible? How many times had I warned junior agents of honey traps? My guard had been down because I was dealing with a bunch of Islamic fundamentalists. I thought they were all anti-women and that no woman would ever work for them. I had neglected the fact that Ayub was no fundamentalist, but only an opportunist. I had fallen into a honey trap, but fortuitously hadn't spilled the beans.

'But the clincher came this morning when we were driving to Basingstoke,' I told Nilofer and Ayub. 'On Ayub's sweater, yes, the blue sweater he is wearing now, I saw a nice long strand of jet black hair. Yes, Nilofer's hair. And then the penny dropped.' By that time Ayub had almost dropped to one knee, and was clutching the bedstead's head for support. I guess my kick to his kneecap earlier in the day did have a material and possibly adverse impact on him.

Ayub looked at me balefully, but kept quiet. 'Ever since I met him for the first time, I've loved him,' Nilofer declared defiantly.

'And why not? There's nothing wrong in that. But you

should not have got involved in this Taliban and al Qaeda business.'

'I did it for my country,' she declared proudly.

'He's brainwashed you into believing that the Taliban will stop fighting Pakistan once they have control over Afghanistan. That they won't try to capture power in Pakistan either. I hope none of Junaid's friends get to know that you both had an affair. Using the Taliban to achieve your political ends is one thing. Using their wives, when they are away, is another.' Nilofer and Ayub were silent. Was it because they saw the light or because they were defeated?

'I assume you sent Junaid outside on some chore last night when you spent some quality time with Nilofer?' I asked Ayub.

'Tell me,' Ayub asked us, refusing to answer my question. 'Why take the trouble of putting us through the Tantalus Test? What did you gain from it?'

'We knew that you would try to call your friends in the local al Qaeda rings and tell them to stop killing Wasim Hunsud's men. We wanted to know who those supporters are. Those numbers you tried to call, they will lead us to a few more people, right?'

I got no response, but Ayub and Nilofer's expressions suggested that I was right. And there would be no stopping the intra-ISI feud in Pakistan.

'At least tell me where you have kept my Old Monk bottles,' I asked Ayub. There was a stony silence.

'That'll be one of the objectives for our interrogators, Ritwik. To find out where this blackguard has kept those three bottles. But why don't you switch to something else for a change? I can offer you some very good Scotch. Or better still, some good Jack Daniels from Tennessee.'

'Thanks but no, General. The Russians did try to get me to switch to vodka, but it never worked.'

'Take them both away,' General West told the bemused SAS men. He then turned to me and asked, 'I'll be driving to the foreign office. Do you want a lift?'

I was silent as I looked out of the window. 'Might as well go with me,' he offered. 'It won't be much fun walking all the way from Mile End to Pall Mall through this slush.'

General West was right. The snow that had smothered the garden had now completely disappeared. The greyish slush that now replaced it didn't look particularly inviting. I got up from bed and silently followed General West out of the room without giving Nilofer a second glance. But I did leave behind a small piece of my heart in that room.

# Epilogue

I WAS IN GOA, RECUPERATING AT A BEACH RESORT WHERE I was the only guest, a crystal glass with a Patiala peg of Old Monk in my hand. My bare feet traced patterns in the sand, as I lay on a deck chair and watched the sunset. It was high tide and the waves were progressively getting closer to my feet. My mobile rang. It was General West. I considered not accepting the call. Hadn't General West promised me that he wouldn't trouble me on any account for an entire month as my body and mind recovered from the treatment received at the hands of Ayub, Junaid and their cohorts? I answered the call with a sigh. If General West was calling me, then it had to be something important.

'Ritwik, you good?' The Ohio accent was still strong, despite the distance.

'I'm fine, General West,' I replied politely. There was silence at the other end. Let him tell me what he wants, I thought. I was darned if I had to make small talk to fill the silence.

'Something interesting happened. I wanted to know what you felt before I made my recommendations.'

'Has the Pakistani government changed its mind about waiving Ayub's diplomatic immunity?'

'Yes, it has. Pakistan no longer insists on trying both Ayub and Rashid Qayyum in Pakistan.'

'How did this happen?'

'We agreed to hold the trial in-camera, without any publicity. The last thing they want is for word to get out that an ISI officer posted in London and a general deputed to the IAG have been working for the al Qaeda.'

'So when will the trial start?' I had a number of questions to ask, most important of which was how Nilofer was getting on in jail.

'Soon. Did you know that Ayub has an uncle who is very high up in the ISI hierarchy?

'Who *was* very high up in the ISI hierarchy. Past tense. That chap's retired now. What about him?'

'He's approached us with a proposal.'

'I presume he doesn't want his darling nephew to serve twenty years at the Belmarsh prison. What's he offering us?'

'In exchange for showing leniency to Ayub Afridi, he has offered to help us locate Al-Kuwaiti.' I whistled softly on hearing that. We had got the name Abu Ahmed Al-Kuwaiti from a Guantanamo detainee a few years ago, but we were yet to find him. One of the two or three people whom Osama bin Laden trusted implicitly, Al-Kuwaiti was the one who carried messages to and from bin Laden to the rest of the al Qaeda.

If we could locate Al Kuwaiti, we would find bin Laden. Not that finding bin Laden mattered so much anymore.

'He knows where Al Kuwaiti is?'

'No, he doesn't. But he knows that Al-Kuwaiti occasionally calls someone and he knows who that someone is.'

'Why didn't he tell us till now? Does he have an explanation for that?'

'Yes. He says that he went shopping for something he could give us, in exchange for his nephew's freedom. He may be speaking the truth. It doesn't matter.'

'How often does Al-Kuwaiti call this someone?'

'Maybe once in six months, maybe eight months.'

'And what have you decided, General West?'

'I wanted to know what you felt. If we let Ayub walk away after say, two years in jail, would he return to the al Qaeda?'

'I doubt it. As long as Ayub was a diplomat and lived comfortably, he didn't mind flying the al Qaeda flag by his side. So do hundreds of ISI officers even now. Now that he has lost his diplomat's status, he is unlikely to want to do grunt work for the brotherhood.'

'That's my sense as well. His uncle lives on a farm in the Swat valley and he promises us that he will keep Ayub by his side and will make sure he gets up to no further mischief.'

We were silent for a minute. Then General West asked, 'So do we accept his offer to give us the name of the man who contacts Al-Kuwaiti?'

'Let's go for it, General. Let's agree with Ayub's uncle that we will let Ayub walk away free after two years in prison, provided we find Al-Kuwaiti by that time on the basis of information provided to us. What do we have to lose? That chap may indeed lead us to Al-Kuwaiti and Al-Kuwaiti could lead us to Osama. Capturing or killing Osama is not going to neutralise the al Qaeda, but it would be a shot in the arm for us. God knows we could do with a good symbolic win!'

'Ayub's uncle, tells us that Section S is in all likelihood keeping bin Laden inside Pakistan, most probably in a big city, somewhere you wouldn't expect to find him.'

I grunted. Section S was an ISI unit which for the record was not part of the ISI, composed of specially selected men who for the sake of keeping appearances had quit the ISI before joining Section S. It went without saying that Section S got involved in a lot of dirty stuff, stuff which the ISI ought not legitimately get involved in. 'Well, we've scoured the tribal belt for bin Laden. If he's there, we should have found him by now. Drones, rewards, we've tried everything.'

There was some more silence. We would know where bin Laden was hiding once we find him. Till then we could sprout as many theories as we wanted on where he was.

'So you agree with my assessment? Good. I'll sign the papers and then if we find Al-Kuwaiti, the Brits will come up with an excuse for letting Ayub go free – good behaviour or something. I won't trouble you any more Ritwik. Enjoy your break. Good—'

'There's one more thing, General...'

'Yes, Ritwik. What's it?'

'Could you possibly show Nilofer some leniency as well once Al-Kuwaiti has been captured? She's totally innocent. She got involved with Ayub because Junaid was so nasty to her and she blindly did whatever Ayub asked her to do.'

'Ayub's uncle hasn't requested us to help Nilofer…' A wave came perilously close to where I was sitting.

'And I'm sure he doesn't give two hoots about her. However, she is a widow and should face no hurdles in marrying Ayub if they both wished, once they complete their jail sentences. There's no reason why Nilofer should stay in jail a day longer than Ayub Afridi.' Munir and small fry like that long-haired driver might spend longer in jail than Ayub, if we accepted Ayub's uncle's offer, but I didn't care.

'Tell you what, Ritwik, you are a softie. You pretend to be a tough cookie but you—'

'I doubt you are any different, General West.'

'Ha! You think so?'

'Is that a Yes, General West?'

'Yes it is. I'll arrange it so that Ayub and Nilofer are let off once we have Al-Kuwaiti.'

'Goodbye, General West.' I hung up since there was nothing more to say.

I wondered whether Ayub would actually marry Nilofer and take her with him to the Swat valley once they were both free. Did he actually love her or did he merely pretend to love her so that he could use her? No one knew that Ayub and Nilofer had had an affair behind Junaid's back. And no one would know as long the trial was held in-camera. They would be safe there, under Ayub's uncle's eye. However, Ayub might not marry Nilofer. If Ayub didn't marry Nilofer, how would she survive? Would she go back to Pakistan on her own? Or would she stay on in the UK? Would we be able to get Al-Kuwaiti? If we did, would we get the big fish we want? I didn't have answers to any of those questions. I took another sip of the Old Monk as a big wave washed over my feet.